# The Tycoon's Kiss

*The Tycoon's Kiss*

**A TAMING OF THE SHEENANS ROMANCE**

JANE PORTER

The Tycoon's Kiss

Copyright © 2014 Jane Porter

Tule Publishing First Printing, January 2016

The Tule Publishing Group, LLC

ALL RIGHTS RESERVED

No part of this book may be used or reproduced in any manner whatsoever without written permission except in the case of brief quotations embodied in critical articles and reviews.

This is a work of fiction. Names, characters, places, and incidents are products of the author's imagination or are used fictitiously. Any resemblance to actual events, locales, organizations or persons, living or dead, is entirely coincidental.

ISBN 978-1-943963-94-2

# DEDICATION

*For Meghan Farrell.*
*You are Wonder Girl.*
*Tule couldn't do what it's doing without you.*
*(And I'd be miserable without a cool Book Girl around!)*

Dear Reader,

If you've read my books before, you know I love connected stories, and have written numerous series featuring families for Harlequin Presents, Grand Central Publishing and Berkley Books. *The Taming of the Sheenan*s, is my brand new series about six brothers from Marietta, Montana and boy oh boy do these men know how to take over a scene and own the room!

The Sheenans are big, tough, rugged men, and as different as the Montana landscape. I launched the series in December with *Christmas at Copper Mountain,* a story about widower Brock Sheenan, the oldest brother, a taciturn rancher and single father who has been alone too long.

Now the series continues with *Tycoon's Kiss*, featuring the 'good' Sheenan twin, venture capitalist Troy, named Marietta's Most Eligible Bachelor by the Copper Mountain Courier several years ago.

But thirty-six year old Troy is more than a pretty face. He's brilliant and ambitious, loyal to his family, and has a secret soft spot for historical buildings, small towns, and brainy book girls.

I hope you'll enjoy Taylor Harris and Troy Sheenan's romance in *Tycoon's Kiss*. These two stole my heart as has all of Marietta. Welcome back to Marietta, Montana nestled beneath majestic Copper Mountain!

Don't miss the other Sheenan stories available now:

Christmas at Copper Mountain (Brock Sheenan's story), The Kidnapped Christmas Bride (Trey Sheenan's story), The Taming of the Bachelor (Dillion Sheenan's story), A Christmas Miracle for Daisy (Cormac Sheenan's story).

*Jane Porter*

# Chapter One

MONTANA WINTERS WERE never mild, and this winter felt even more brutal than normal.

Taylor Harris sucked in a sharp breath at the blast of frigid air as she and Jane Weiss, the new director of the Marietta Chamber of Commerce, stepped from the warm library into the night.

The frigid temperature and biting wind made her eyes water behind her glasses. Taylor fumbled with her key, blinking as she struggled to get Marietta library's front door locked. She had to remove her mitten to punch in the security code on the wall.

Jane stood close by, shoulders hunched, teeth chattering. "You're sure you don't mind driving me to the airport?" she asked, drawing her suitcase closer to her feet.

"Of course not," Taylor answered, shivering as she quickly tugged her mitten back on. Normally she'd be racing home on a night like this for a hot bath, a steaming cup of soup, and a great book in bed. Taylor had been a book lover her entire life and even at twenty-six, loved nothing more than curling up and getting lost in a great story, reading until the early hours of the morning. So what if it meant she never got enough sleep? Books were her life, her passion. It's why she'd become a librarian.

They set off for the broad, pale stone steps that led to the park and parking lot, Jane's roller bag bumped along next to them.

Taylor glanced across Crawford Park to the tall, domed courthouse dominating the public park. Even though it was only a few minutes after six, the sky was already dark and the yellow glow of street lamps reflected off the snow heaped onto the sides of the city park's paths. Larger, dirtier piles of snow lined Marietta's streets, thanks to the diligent efforts of the city's snow plows, and now a new storm was predicted to move in tonight, which would mean even bigger piles tomorrow.

Jane glanced anxiously up at the sky. "It's supposed to start snowing later. You're okay driving in a storm?"

Taylor nodded, smiling, amused. "Of course. I'm from northeastern Montana. All we do is drive in snow and ice. It's you I'm worried about. You think your flight will get out okay?"

"I checked with the airline. So far, so good, and I have those alerts on my phone so I'll know right away if there's a change in status." Jane lifted her bag, carrying it down the salted front steps, slightly breathless by the time they reached

THE TYCOON'S KISS

the sidewalk. "So what are you wearing to the ball Friday?"

Taylor knew the Valentine Ball would come up, and she dreaded breaking the news to Jane that she'd decided not to attend. "I wanted to talk to you about that," she said carefully. "I've—"

"Don't. Don't say you've changed your mind. You promised me!"

Taylor hated disappointing anyone, much less the best friend she'd made since moving to Marietta six months ago, but Jane enjoyed big events and Taylor did not. "It's just not my thing, Jane, and it's incredibly expensive—"

"You're getting a free ticket for being on the Wedding Giveaway committee."

Taylor adjusted her red and brown striped scarf around her neck, trying in vain to block the wind. "Things have been stressful with Doug and all the changes at the library. I'd honestly rather stay home and unwind. I've got a new book by one of my favorite authors—"

"You can read over the weekend. You don't need to spend your Friday night in bed!"

"Why not?" Taylor exclaimed, as they darted across the parking lot. "We both know I'm not a ball kind of girl. I'm a librarian. And boring as mud. Trust me, you'll have more fun without me."

Jane raced next to Taylor, teeth chattering again. "You're only boring because you don't go out and do anything!"

"I like being home. I like reading."

3

Jane shuddered as the freezing wind whipped past. "You're too young to become a hermit."

Taylor peeled a long strand of hair from her lashes and tugged her knit cap lower on her head. "I'm not a hermit. I'm just an introvert, which means I like people, but I don't find parties exciting. They tire me out—."

"You sound like an old lady!" Jane interrupted, giggling. "But you're young and beautiful and this is a once in a lifetime event. A historic event to commemorate the 100 year anniversary of Marietta's 1914 Great Wedding Giveaway—" she broke off and glanced up at the sky as the first slow, lazy snowflakes drifted down. "It's starting to snow."

"We'll get you to the airport," Taylor said. "You'll make it."

Jane dragged her bag across an icy patch. "So when does it warm up?"

"May? June?"

"*No!*"

"Don't think about it," Taylor said, as they arrived at her car and she clicked the unlock button on her key ring. "It'll just make it worse."

Inside the car, as Taylor turned the engine on, Jane held her hands to one of the vents, waiting for the heat to kick in. "You have to come, Taylor. It's the party of the century. Everyone's going to be there—." she broke off, frowned, hesitated. "Okay, from the sluggish ticket sales, we know not *everyone* will be at the Graff Hotel Friday night, but most of

Crawford County's movers and shakers will. It's going to be beautiful. Don't you want to see the ballroom decorated?"

"I do. That's why I've volunteered to help Risa deliver the flowers Friday. But that's enough for me. I love to read about balls in my Regency romances, but there's nothing in me begging to go to a ball. Besides, even if I went, what would I wear?"

"That's easy. I'll take you shopping, and Taylor, you have to go. We're sitting at the Sheenan table. It'd be rude to not go now."

Taylor backed out from the parking spot, shifted into drive. "Just have catering remove a place setting and chair from the table. No one will even notice if there is eight, nine, or ten at the table."

"Yes, they will."

"No, they won't."

"Yes. They will." Jane exhaled hard before adding in a small voice, "Because you're Troy Sheenan's date."

"*What?*" Taylor slammed on her brakes and stared at Jane.

"He just broke up with his girlfriend and he needed a date and you didn't have a date so I told him–"

"No, you did not."

"I did."

"Why would you do that?"

"He's really nice."

"No he's not. You said he broke your heart."

"Okay, nice is maybe the wrong word. But he is seriously gorgeous and sexy and smart. Very, very smart. And successful. Rich as Midas—"

"Jane, no. He sounds awful. Yuck. *No.*"

"It's just for the ball. You can go with Mitch and me. We'll drive you home. And I promise that Troy won't make a move—"

"*No.*"

"Although he is by far the best kisser—"

"Don't care. Don't want to know." Taylor's hands tightened on the steering wheel as she moved her foot from the brake to the gas pedal. "And you agreed after that last terrible set up that you wouldn't put me through anymore blind dates." She shot Jane a severe look. "I'm holding you to that promise, Jane."

Jane slunk down in her seat. "I'm not asking you to marry him, just be his date."

Taylor said nothing, her gaze narrowed and focused on the road.

"Normally I wouldn't set him up. I wouldn't want to see him with another woman but you're not… plastic… and you wouldn't be into him for his money…" Jane's voice drifted off. She shifted uncomfortably in her seat. Silence followed.

Taylor clamped her jaw tight.

She was not interested in going to the ball, and definitely not interested in being set up with gorgeous, rich, sexy Troy

Sheenan, Jane's ex-love, whom Taylor had heard *far* too much about over the past few months.

Good Lord. From everything Jane had said, Troy was a handsome, ruthless, self-absorbed playboy. Could anything be worse?

"You'd enjoy talking to him," Jane said faintly, hands knotting in her lap. "He's very smart—brilliant, really—and exceedingly well read. You should see his personal library—"

"*Jane.*"

"He's just got his hands full with his break up, his dad dying, and hosting the ball for us in his hotel. It's a massive expense that he personally is underwriting."

Taylor flexed her fingers against the steering wheel. "That's not my problem, and it's not yours, either."

"I know, but I offered to help—"

"Wait. You offered to set him up? He didn't ask you?"

"No."

"Oh, Jane." Taylor sighed. "You're still in love with him."

Jane's head bowed. "I know we're not going to be together. And I'm moving on, I am, but that doesn't mean I can't care for Troy, and it doesn't mean I can't want him to be happy."

Taylor just shook her head. She'd been in Jane's shoes once, back when she was in graduate school, and it was a bad place to be. Unrequited love was brutal. All those intense emotions, bottled up inside, making your feelings strong, too strong. "You need to let him go. Completely."

For a long moment Jane said nothing, and then she sighed heavily. "So what do I tell Troy?"

Taylor rolled her eyes. "To be a man and go find his own damn date."

TROY SHEENAN WAS glad to be on the ground, even if he was arriving in the middle of a blizzard. He was a seasoned traveler, accustomed to jetting back and forth between Montana and California to oversee the renovations at the Graff Hotel during the last couple of years, but tonight's flight was rough. Seriously rough. Three endless, unrelenting hours of turbulence that kept him buckled into his leather seat, as the pilots of his private jet searched in vain for some smoother air.

They didn't find it.

But at least he and his crew were safely on the ground and he was free to move, his long strides carrying him swiftly across the snowy tarmac to the executive terminal.

His rental car, a big black four wheel drive SUV with snow tires, was waiting for him outside the executive terminal, the key already in the ignition, the interior still warm. The paperwork had been handled earlier by Troy's assistant before he left San Francisco which meant he was free to go.

Troy tossed his bags into the back, and slid behind the steering wheel, noting that the snow flurries were coming down thicker and faster. In good weather it was at least a fifty-five minute drive to Sheenan Ranch. And it wasn't good weather. He wasn't even sure if Dillon would have been able to get their private drive plowed, which meant he might be four wheeling it. Or stuck.

Any other night he'd just stay at the hotel. He had his own private suite on the fourth floor of the historic hotel, and the suite was always kept ready for him, but if Dad was doing as badly as Dillon said, Troy wanted to get to the ranch tonight and sit with him. Troy hadn't been there when his mom died, and he was damn well not going to be MIA when Dad passed.

THE SNOW WAS really coming down now.

Taylor sat ramrod straight in the driver's seat, her hands set precisely at ten and two on the steering wheel, her heart pounding harder than she liked.

She wasn't scared.

She'd driven through worse.

And the road seemed fine, not too icy. She just had to keep an eye on her speed and pay attention.

And yes, it was getting harder and harder to see the hood of her car, never mind the road, but she was a Montana girl. She had a good car, a reliable car, and her Subaru could handle the icy roads just fine.

The car would be fine, and she'd be fine, she silently insisted, even as she regretted that she hadn't stopped in Bozeman when she had the chance.

She should have not pushed it. She should have played it safe. But Taylor had thought that maybe the flurries would lighten. She'd thought perhaps once she hit the highway the storm would ease.

She'd thought wrong and now she was driving through a blinding sheet of white, having to pretend her pulse wasn't racing and her hands weren't damp against the steering wheel.

Fifteen more miles, she told herself, checking the windshield wiper speed again. But they were already on their fastest setting and unable to clear her windshield quickly enough.

She couldn't see.

*It's okay.*

She hated this.

*You're halfway home.*

Her eyes burned as she fought panic. She wanted to pull over, get off the road but this was a mountain pass and it'd be suicide to pull over here. Another motorist or trucker could lose control and take her out.

No choice but to keep going. No choice but to finish what she'd started.

And so she sat tall and held her breath and focused very hard on the glow of white where the car headlights shone through the swirling flurries of snow, unable to reach as far as the yellow reflectors on the side of the road. Taylor only knew for sure where she was when she drove over one of the bumps.

Too far right. She was practically on the shoulder. Not good.

She corrected, steering a little more to the left, frowning hard, trying to see the road, knowing it curved somewhere near here, a fairly sharp curve which wasn't a problem during the day but could be treacherous at night. She was concentrating very hard on staying off the reflector bumps and in the middle of her lane when suddenly a row of red lights glowed. It was a big rig truck hitting its brakes.

Taylor hadn't even known a vehicle was in front of her, and she slammed on her brakes to avoid rear-ending it, which put her in a skid on the ice.

Braking hard on ice was the absolute wrong thing to do. She was supposed to pump the brakes, supposed to keep the brakes from locking. Too late.

Her tires spun, and her car spun, and she went careening off the shoulder before slamming violently into the metal side guard.

Her airbag deployed, the impact knocking the air from her.

Taylor knew she'd stopped moving when everything grew still and quiet. She sat for a moment, dazed, barely able to see over the airbag.

Cautiously, she opened her door and stepped out into the snow. She shivered as she inspected her car where it had slammed into the guardrail. The guardrail was twisted and bent, but it had stopped her car from going over the edge.

Good guardrail.

"That was close," a deep male voice said from behind her. "You alright?"

"I think so," she answered, swaying a bit as she turned around. A man was walking towards her, his big SUV parked just behind her car, his headlamps on high beams to illuminate the highway shoulder. "Just shaken up more than anything."

The man walked past her, took a look at the guardrail and crushed hood, before returning. "That guardrail saved you."

"I know."

"What happened?"

"The truck in front of me slammed on its brakes, and I had nowhere to go."

"You were following it too closely?"

"I didn't even know it was there."

He nodded. "It's bad. Total white out conditions. None of us should be on the road."

"I just wanted to get home."

"Where were you heading?"

"Marietta."

"That's where I'm going. Let me give you a ride."

Taylor glanced back at his big black SUV with the headlights shining on them. It looked like a new car, and expensive. She gave him the same once-over. He looked expensive, too. Clean cut. Attractive, with black hair, smooth hard jaw, strong, classic features. "Are you safe?" she asked, only half joking.

"Safer than the storm."

"Not sure that's hugely reassuring."

He laughed, the sound deep, warm as well as very confident. "Sorry. Let me introduce myself." He stuck out a hand and smiled down on her, white teeth glinting, and creases fanning at the corners of his eyes. "I'm Troy Sheenan."

# Chapter Two

OF COURSE HE was, Taylor thought, adjusting the seatbelt across her lap, and then crossing her leg at the knee, trying to make herself comfortable in the big black SUV's passenger seat.

And of course it would be Troy Sheenan who'd plucked her from the side of the road, as if he were a gallant knight, instead of an errant knight.

A playboy.

A *rake*.

It felt satisfying to silently hurl names at him, but it wasn't helping make her more comfortable. She couldn't relax. Couldn't catch her breath.

It was his fault. *Troy Sheenan.*

Taylor's fingers curled into her palms. She stared blindly out the windshield into the night with the thick swirling snow, her chest tight, aching with bottled air.

Of all people to stop…

Of all people to offer to help.

THE TYCOON'S KISS

Why did it have to be him?

And worse, why couldn't he be arrogant, and rude, and absolutely despicable? *Dislikable?* Why did he have to be almost... charming?

*Nice.*

She shuddered inwardly, thinking that he might even be disarmingly nice, if he weren't, well, so...good looking. Jane hadn't lied about that. He was...well, exactly what she'd said he was.

Tall, dark and handsome...black hair, blue eyes, chiseled jaw, dimples.

A man with all those attributes couldn't be nice. Truly handsome men were never nice. They were spoiled, overly confident, *insincere.* They were accustomed to women falling to their feet and throwing themselves at them, bosoms heaving... and so forth.

Taylor's lips compressed and she lifted her chin a fraction.

She couldn't place all the blame on handsome men. Women had to accept some responsibility for their behavior. Just because a man was gorgeous and charming it didn't mean a woman needed to fall for him...

Taylor would *never* fall for someone like Troy Sheenan.

At least, she'd never fall for someone like Troy Sheenan again.

Back in graduate school she'd fallen for a Mr. Charming, and it had broken her heart and damaged her confidence and self-esteem. She'd vowed to never go down that destructive, confusing path again. And she hadn't.

She wouldn't.

She pushed up her glasses higher on the bridge of her nose, suddenly grateful she'd worn them to work today, feeling protected by the big dark frames and the too-thick-to-be-sexy lenses.

She wasn't a plaything, or an intellectual lightweight. Yes, she loved historical romances, and had ever since she'd first read Jane Austen in high school, and then found a Georgette Heyer novel in the local library during her summer vacation. By the time Taylor had graduated with a Masters in Library Science, she'd read everything Heyer wrote (even the mysteries), including a biography just published on the English novelist, and Heyer's work ethic, intelligence, and drive made an indelible impression on Taylor. If Heyer could support her family with her writing in the 1920's and 30's, then Taylor could support her brother with her work.

Taylor didn't need a man or husband to provide. Taylor would provide. And she had. Which reminded her, she'd need to call her insurance agent as soon as she reached the house, and a tow truck, and make arrangements for a rental car. She sighed inwardly, disappointed in herself for losing control on the pass. There were a lot of things going on this week. She didn't need the hassle of being car-less on top of everything else.

Leaning forward, she reached for her oversized leather satchel at her feet. Taylor didn't use purses. She loved her messenger-style book bag and she quickly found the satchel's inner pocket where she kept her phone. Retrieving it, she checked messages but there was no service. They'd get service when they got closer to Marietta and that wouldn't be long now.

"You said you were new in town," Troy said, his deep, low voice breaking the silence.

She nodded as his dark blue gaze briefly slid over her in the dim light of the car before his gaze returned to the road.

She exhaled, hard.

He'd only looked at her for a moment but it was enough to make her insides flip, setting loose a dozen butterflies in her middle. She pressed her phone to her lap, and drew a deep breath to calm the nervous butterflies. "I moved to Marietta at the end of August, right before Labor Day weekend."

"What do you think of the place?"

"I like it."

"People nice?"

She thought of Judge McCorkle and how he'd handled the sentencing of her brother. She thought also of those who'd been so critical towards Jane and her ideas for the Chamber of Commerce. "Most people."

He shot her another swift glance. "You've met some less than friendly folks?"

There went the butterflies again. She shifted, uneasy. She didn't understand it, didn't understand why he'd make her feel so nervous, but every time he looked at her, every time she met his gaze, her heart raced.

So strange.

Men didn't give her the jitters. And polished, sophisticated men, especially handsome sophisticated men, didn't appeal to her. She wasn't a fan of city men, finding them too smooth, too slick. But even in his dark wool trousers and expensive black cashmere V-neck sweater, Troy exuded strength. Toughness. He had a rugged masculinity that was pure Montana.

Maybe that's what she was reacting to.

If so, she needed to stop. She didn't want to be attracted to Troy Sheenan. And maybe it wasn't really Troy. Maybe it was the accident. Maybe she was still in shock, shaken from the impact, disoriented from spinning on the ice and slamming into the guardrail. Yes, that was it. The accident. She was still shaken up. Relief rushed through her. Everything made sense now. "Most people have been polite to me," she said carefully. "But that's not necessarily true for others. It seems like there are different standards in Marietta. If you are from Marietta, there is one set of rules, and if you're new to Marietta, there's another."

"Can you give me specifics?"

"I don't know that I should. I don't want to criticize your hometown. Suffice it to say, there are some in the community that view newcomers with suspicion, particularly if they're suggesting change. But that is probably true for most small towns. I'm from a small Montana town myself, an hour from Scoby. Hopeville—"

"Hopeville?" he repeated.

She grimaced. "Has to be ironic. There wasn't much *hope* in Hopeville. Our population was less than a thousand and there was no opportunity there, nor much of anything but hard drinking and hard living."

"How did you end up in Marietta?"

"A job," she said.

"What do you do?"

She primly adjusted her glasses. "I'm a librarian."

"You are?"

She heard the note of surprise in his voice, as well as a measure of respect. "I've been hired to take over as head librarian when Margaret Houghton retires in June," she added, feeling a small bubble of warmth. She was proud of her position. She loved her work as a librarian and Marietta's graceful, historic building deserved excellent, modern programs, programs Taylor was determined to implement as soon as she took over.

He shot her a quick, assessing glance. "Impressive."

Taylor's insides felt fluttery all over again. She shouldn't care what he thought. But apparently some part of her— some ridiculous, weak part of her—did.

Annoyed with herself, Taylor stared out her passenger

window, noting how the delicate icy flakes stuck to the glass and wondering how she could bring up Jane without making it awkward.

It might not be possible as just sitting next to Troy was making her feel hopelessly awkward.

Even now her pulse raced and her mouth tasted cotton dry, so she gave up trying to figure out how to introduce the subject of Jane Weiss and focused instead on the snow.

It was beautiful, all those thick, whirling, white flakes. Taylor loved the snow and didn't mind the long winters provided she didn't have to do a lot of driving on mountain passes during storms. Thank goodness Troy Sheenan was comfortable behind the wheel. It was obvious he'd grown up driving in snow and ice, too.

"Have family in Marietta?" he asked, a few minutes later.

She pictured her brother, remembering how they'd moved to Marietta together, or how he'd moved with her after she'd gotten hired by the library. Doug was able to get a job, too, as an apprentice to a Marietta electrician but within weeks of arriving in Marietta, he got in trouble and it'd been difficult ever since.

"Not in town, but in Paradise Valley," Taylor said. "My little brother lives—" she broke off, frowning, uncertain how to explain Doug's situation. She was protective of her brother's illness. Not everyone understood depression and mood disorders. Not everyone wanted to understand. Her own parents had thought his diagnosis was a cop-out. More

THE TYCOON'S KISS

than once Dad had ripped into Doug for being weak and undisciplined. He just couldn't accept that the depression was anything but laziness and selfishness. She gave her head a small shake, shaking away the memory of all the horrible things her parents had said to Doug when he began to struggle in middle school.

She felt, rather than saw, Troy glance at her.

Taylor swallowed and squared her shoulders. "–out there, in Paradise Valley."

"I was raised in Paradise Valley. That's where our family ranch is," Troy said.

Jane had told her about the big Sheenan spread in Paradise Valley, one of the larger ranches in the area, and it bordered the Carrigan property, the other big ranch. Taylor knew Sage Carrigan as Sage was on the Great Wedding Giveaway committee, and was donating all the chocolates and truffles for Friday's Valentine Ball.

The ball.

Right.

Taylor prayed Troy had no idea that she was the one Jane had volunteered to be his date. But then, Taylor doubted Troy had a clue. Men listened to women as little as possible. "Beautiful land," she said.

"Your brother's a cowboy?" Troy asked.

"He's… working on a ranch now, yes," Taylor answered, thinking this was exactly what she didn't want to discuss. She was so private about Doug's situation, and so protective of

21

him. He'd been doing better in the year before they moved here, and they'd both been excited about going to Marietta. It had seemed like a great opportunity for both of them, but Doug couldn't find a job right away, and even though he had time on his hands, he wasn't able to make new friends. Within weeks his depression returned. Taylor had been making calls to psychiatrists in Bozeman at the time Doug was arrested. Sentencing him to a halfway house/rehab ranch wasn't the solution. Doug needed counseling, treatment. *Medical* care. But the judge didn't listen. The judge thought he knew best. He was a man, after all. He claimed he knew what a young man needed. Work. Discipline. *An attitude adjustment.*

The very same things Taylor's father had said.

It made her furious. And heartsick. Because both men were wrong. And Doug—as well as thousands of young men and women—continued to struggle and suffer because people were ignorant about mood disorders.

"You sound unsure," Troy said.

Her lips pursed. Troy was perceptive. She had to be careful what she told him, determined to protect Doug as much as possible. "The ranch life is new to him," she said after a slight hesitation. "It's an adjustment."

"Ranching is hard work."

True, and Doug was never supposed to be a ranch hand. He'd gone to school to be an electrician. He was smart and good with his hands, and was very patient with complicated things. He could succeed. He just needed support. He needed someone to give him a chance. But people didn't want to hire young adults with problems. Taylor was discovering that too many people didn't want to be troubled by other people's problems, which made her worry about the future. She worried about Doug being able to have the future he wanted and deserved.

"The physical work isn't the issue," she said after a moment, picking her words carefully, not sure if Troy was friends with the owners of Hogue Ranch. In a small town, you could never be too careful. "It's the... environment. It's not the best place for him."

"What would be better for him?"

"He wanted to be an electrician. He took all the courses and passed all these tests. He just needs to be given a chance, an apprenticeship. And it'll happen. It will."

"So the ranch is just a stepping stone to the next job," Troy said.

"Yes." She smiled, wanting to believe it. Needing to believe it. She loved Doug dearly. It had about killed her going away to college and leaving her younger brother behind with parents who refused to understand not just who Doug was, but what he needed. "That's right."

They lapsed again into silence but this time neither of them tried to fill it.

Troy's powerful four wheel drive made quick work of the mountain pass.

"Almost there," Troy said a little bit later, putting on his turn signal, as they approached the exit for Marietta. It was still snowing, but the flurries were lighter and the snow plows had been working all evening, keeping the city roads clear. "Which part of town do you live?"

"Near downtown, ten blocks north of the library on Bramble Lane."

"Know that street well. I had a girlfriend in high school that lived on Bramble," he said, smiling crookedly, "and one of my best friends, Mason Jones, lived there, too."

"I'm renting a room from the Jones'."

"Then I know right where to go."

Minutes later he was pulling up in front of the one and a half story Victorian home, the pale yellow paint contrasted with lots of creamy white trim, and snow. Mounds of snow. The snow clung to the big evergreen in the corner of the yard and blanketed the shrubs and hedges lining the front walk.

"So his parents rented you a room," Troy said, shifting into park.

"His sister, Kara, did. She bought the house from her parents when they wanted to move to Florida."

"Kara was just a pipsqueak when I knew her."

"She's not a pipsqueak anymore." Taylor leaned forward and reached for her leather satchel. "She's a Crawford County district attorney."

"Is she, really?" Troy grinned. "Good for her. Tell her

THE TYCOON'S KISS

hello from me. Not sure she'll remember me—"

"She remembers you." Taylor couldn't forget how Kara had positively *gushed* when talking to Jane about the Sheenan brothers during the Chamber's Christmas party. Apparently Jane wasn't the only Troy Sheenan fan in Marietta. "And I'll tell her hello," she added, reaching for the door handle. "Thanks for the ride."

"Glad I could help. And if you need help tomorrow—"

"I'll be fine," she said quickly, opening the door to slide out of the car. She swiftly shouldered her bag and shuddered at the blast of cold air.

"You never did tell me your name," Troy called to her.

Taylor tugged on her scarf, and forced a smile. "Taylor. Taylor Harris."

He laughed softly. "I thought so."

"You did?"

He nodded, his expression amused. "Jane told me all about you."

Taylor suddenly couldn't breathe. "She did?"

"You're my date Friday night."

TROY SAW TAYLOR Harris's eyes widen and her lips part in surprise for a split second before her mouth shut.

She managed a few words, mostly incomprehensible words and then raced up the walkway to the Jones' front door. He stayed put, waiting for her to unlock the door. Once she was safely inside, he shifted into drive and pulled away.

So that was Taylor Harris, the new librarian.

Interesting.

He'd known Jane had set him up with Marietta's new librarian, but he hadn't expected Taylor Harris to be such a fiery, prickly little thing, nor had he expected her enormous tortoise frame glasses. The glasses practically covered her face.

Troy wondered why Jane would set him up with Taylor for the ball.

Troy did like smart women, but Taylor Harris wasn't anything like the women he dated. He preferred urban sophisticates, women that were very ambitious and success-ful… lawyers, doctors, executives, entrepreneurs. Ever since graduating from college, he'd been drawn to women who had big careers and big lives, women who didn't depend on a man and knew how to take care of themselves. Women who preferred to take care of themselves. Independence was sexy. Intelligence and passion was sexy.

But the ball was just one night, he told himself. And Jane insisted that he needed a date, as it wouldn't be proper to attend a black-tie ball at his own hotel without someone gorgeous on his arm.

Troy's brow furrowed as he pictured the petite brunette who'd sat in his passenger seat staring out the window.

He'd never in a million years call her gorgeous.

He wouldn't even describe her as pretty. But she wasn't

THE TYCOON'S KISS

homely, either.

Without her glasses she might be very attractive…

He sighed, wishing he hadn't let Jane talk him into setting him up. He hadn't felt the need to take anyone to the ball. His brother Dillon would be there, and so far Dillon hadn't asked anyone to be his date. Cormac was supposed to be flying in from California to see Dad and attend the ball, and Cormac wasn't sure if he'd have a date. The only Sheenan who had a date at this point, was Brock, and he was bringing his fiancée Harley.

But you have a date now, he reminded himself, and it was the perfect date for him since Troy didn't do long distance relationships and he wasn't about to get involved with someone in Marietta.

Much less Marietta's new prickly librarian.


As Troy approached the old, two story ranch house twenty-five minutes later, the SUV's snow tires crunching gravel, snow and ice, he noticed that the house was dark except for a light downstairs in the back.

Parking in front, Troy left his bags in the truck, and headed inside. He was eager to see his brother and dad.

The front door was unlocked as always and Troy walked down the hall to the kitchen where the light was shining. Thirty year old Dillon was at the farmhouse style sink, washing dishes.

"How's Dad tonight?" Troy asked, as Dillon caught sight

27

of him and turned the water off.

Dillon grabbed a towel and dried his hands. "Better, now that he's sleeping."

"I saw your text. He had a rough day?"

"He was upset today. He wants to go to the cemetery." Dillon paused, glanced at Troy. "See Mom's grave."

Troy's forehead creased. "Mom's not buried in town."

"I know."

"Her ashes are here."

"I *know*." Dillon tossed the towel onto the counter. "I told Dad that but he got all fired up, snapped at me that I was being disrespectful and to just do what he asked me to do." He shook his head. "Hard to see him like this. He was always so tough. Now he's like a lost little kid."

"Or a grouchy little kid."

Dillon smiled. "Glad you're back. It's good to see you."

"Why don't you get out of here? Go into town. I'll sit with Dad tonight."

"It's getting late, and snowing pretty good."

"It's not even nine and you drive one badass truck. You'll be fine."

"You really want to get rid of me."

"I really want you to have a break. You've been alone with Dad for weeks—"

"Not that long. Harley's been coming over almost every day for a couple hours at a time and then yesterday Brock came with her and the kids and they spent the day here so I

THE TYCOON'S KISS

could get out, and take care of some banking and shopping. When I came home, she had dinner all made."

"So why hasn't Brock married her?"

"I don't know, but I'm thinking I should nominate them Friday night for that wedding giveaway contest. Can't think of anyone around here more deserving."

"True," Troy agreed. "But now, go, get out of here while you can. If you leave now, you could be at Grey's by nine thirty, shooting the shit, playing pool, and flirting with all those girls who have a thing for you."

"All those pretty girls in tight jeans and short skirts are looking for a husband. And I'm happy playing darts and having a beer and making out in my truck, but that's as far as it goes. I'm not looking to settle down, and nowhere near ready to be married."

"That makes two of us," Troy said, before heading upstairs to the master bedroom tucked back under the steep eaves of the eighty year old cabin, the interior walls covered with paneling, to hide the rustic split log walls.

For the next two hours Troy sat by the side of his father's bed in the house that had been home to three generations of Sheenans, and tried not to think.

Or feel.

But that was easier done if he didn't look at his father, who was now just a frail version of himself.

Easier done if Troy had remained in San Francisco, on task in his office on the thirtieth floor in the city's financial district, or in his sprawling home in exclusive, affluent Pacific Heights with its views of the Golden Gate Bridge, Alcatraz and the Bay.

But Troy had come home, and he'd returned for this. To be here. To take some of the pressure from Dillon's shoulders, and ensure that his father was as comfortable as possible in the coming weeks.

Dillon had warned him Dad was fading, but even then it was a shock for Troy to see how much his father had changed since Christmas. His father didn't even look like the same person.

It had always been hard for Troy to return to Marietta. He didn't like coming home, didn't like the memories or emotions, and that was before Dad was sick.

Now…

He shook his head, his jaw tight.

Now he just felt even angrier, but Trey was the angry Sheenan. Trey was the one who drank too much and hit things, broke things. Not Troy.

But whenever Troy did return to Marietta, and the ranch, he felt an awful lot like his infamous twin who was currently spending a five year sentence in jail.

Troy shifted uncomfortably in the antique chair positioned close to the bed, thinking if they were going to continue these bedside vigils for their dad, who was clearly on the downward slope now, then they really needed to get a bigger, sturdier chair in the bedroom.

THE TYCOON'S KISS

Footsteps sounded in the hall and floorboards creaked as Dillon entered the dimly lit master bedroom.

"You're back," Troy said.

"Had a couple beers and nearly got into a fight with a punchy little cowboy acting like an asshole around Callan, but Grey threw me out before I could teach that boy some manners."

"You and Callan dating?"

"Callan and me? God, no. I've known her since she was in diapers but we are pretty tight. We have fun together," Dillon said, running a hand through his thick dark hair, his hair the same shade as Troy's, Trey's and Brock's. Only Cormac was fair, the same dark blond their dad had been in his early thirties. The rest of the Sheenan boys took after their late mother, Jeanette, who'd been part Indian, part Irish, and one hundred percent beautiful.

One hundred percent beautiful, and two hundred percent crazy.

Troy stretched out his legs, crossing his boots at the ankle. No, that wasn't fair. Mom wasn't crazy. She'd just been terribly lonely and unhappy on the ranch.

It hadn't been the life she wanted, isolated from town and friends, alone except for her husband and her five sons.

Dad should have insisted she learn how to drive.

Dad should have insisted she got into town.

Dad should have taken care of her better.

Troy clamped his jaw, teeth grinding. Or they, her sons,

should have, he thought, glancing up at Dillon.

Shouldn't her boys have done more? Because isn't that what sons should do? Take care of their mother?

"How was Dad while I was gone?" Dillon asked.

"He got up once, needing to use the bathroom, and I helped him get there, but the rest of the time, he pretty much slept."

Dillon leaned against one of the columns of the four poster bed. "He does that a lot."

"He thought I was Trey," Troy added.

"Understandable, you're twins and Trey used to live here with him."

"He insisted I was Trey."

Dillon grinned. "So what did you do?"

"Act like I was Trey, and let him lecture me on how I needed to make things right with McKenna and step up and take responsibility for my son."

Dillon's smile faded. "Yeah, well, that's not going to happen."

"Trey loves his son, and McKenna."

"Kind of hard to be a good partner and father in jail."

"He'll get out and he'll get his act together."

"Yeah, but it'll be too late by then, at least, for him and McKenna."

Troy's brows pulled. "You think so?"

Dillon grimaced. "She's getting married again."

"*What?*"

THE TYCOON'S KISS

Dillon nodded. "Lawrence proposed last week, after asking Rory and Quinn for permission to marry their sister. Of course, Rory and Quinn, who both hate Trey, said yes."

"If McKenna was our sister we'd hate Trey, too," Troy said quietly, tiredly, aware that Trey would not take the news well. It was a good thing Trey was in jail. Because if Trey *weren't* locked up, there's no way in hell he'd let McKenna, his first and only love, and the mother of his boy, marry another man.

"Who's going to tell Trey?"

"When's the wedding?"

"Not until fall."

"Then there's no point saying anything now. Something could happen. The engagement could get called off. Why work Trey up when it could be nothing?" Troy nodded at the bed. "I'm going to grab my stuff from the truck and crash. I'll see you in the morning."

# Chapter Three

TROY HAD GONE to his truck without his coat and it was cold, seriously cold. His breath clouded in the air as he quickly scooped his bags from the backseat of the big Escalade. He was just about to slam the door shut when he heard a buzzing sound from beneath the passenger seat in front of him.

It sounded an awful lot like a phone.

His heart sank, thinking it was either the little librarian's phone, or the person who'd rented the car before him. Either way it meant that someone, somewhere was without a phone—modern society's lifeline—and probably frustrated as all hell.

Troy opened the passenger door, felt beneath the seat and then the side of the seat by the center console. Found it.

He glanced at the screen with the photo of a young Taylor Harris with a blond teenage boy wearing a high school graduation cap and gown.

Must be Taylor's brother, even as he noted the five

THE TYCOON'S KISS

missed calls, and text after text.

*Not doing so good.*

*Need to talk to you.*

*Call me.*

*Why won't you answer?*

Troy's brow creased, concerned. This didn't sound good at all.

He glanced at the time on the phone's display. It was quarter past eleven. If he drove the phone back to Marietta, he wouldn't arrive until close to midnight. How could he knock on the Jones' front door at midnight?

But then, reading the desperate texts, how could he not?

Troy returned to the house for his coat and wallet. He told Dillon he'd found a phone in the car and had to return it to town. Dillon suggested Troy just stay in town at the hotel. No reason to drive all the way back so late.

Troy thought it made sense and said goodnight, letting his brother know he'd be back before noon to spend the afternoon with Dad.

TAYLOR WOKE UP to Kara clicking the light on in Taylor's bedroom. "You've got a visitor," Kara said, covering her yawn.

"What time is it?" Taylor asked.

"Eleven forty-five."

Taylor's mind cleared, and she sat up abruptly, immedi-

35

ately thinking of Doug as she groped for her glasses on the nightstand. "My brother?" she asked, settling her glasses onto the bridge of her nose.

"No." Kara pushed a tangle of dark blonde hair back from her face, tucking it behind her ear. "Your knight in shining armor. Troy Sheenan." She saw Taylor's baffled expression and added, "You didn't even have to track him down in the morning. He found your phone in his car and has brought it back."

Relief flooded Taylor. She'd discovered she'd lost her phone minutes after Troy had left and didn't know how to reach him without calling Jane, and Taylor didn't have Jane's number memorized, just saved on her phone. "It's awfully late to return it, though," she said, pushing back the covers and swinging her legs over the side of the bed.

Kara shrugged. "Apparently he was worried about some of the messages. He thought they might be... urgent."

"From Doug?" Taylor asked, immediately on her feet and reaching for her thick fleece robe from the foot of the bed.

"Sounds like it."

Rattled, Taylor stuffed her arms into the sleeves and tied the belt around her waist. What had happened? Was Doug in trouble? Had he gotten into it with someone? He'd been beaten up once at Hogue Ranch and he'd vowed he wouldn't walk away from a fight the next time. He'd defend himself...even though it'd mean legal complications.

THE TYCOON'S KISS

Taylor hated the cold queasy uneasiness filling her. She hated that just hearing her brother's name made her worry. Worry was a terrible feeling, and it seemed like she lived in a perpetual state of anxiety over Doug these past six months. She needed him to get better. She needed him to get the right help and then maybe, just maybe, he'd have confidence again. Hope again. As it was, he struggled to hang in there.

But no matter how dark things seemed, she wouldn't give up on him. There was no reason to give up. Doug was young and still physically maturing and as doctors said, a young male's frontal cortex didn't even finish developing until mid-twenties. Doug just needed to be patient. He just needed to believe in himself, the way she believed in him. He'd already survived six months at Hogue. There were just three months left. Once he completed the program, he could live with her. That was the goal. That was the focus. That was her promise to him.

"Where is Troy?" she asked, combing her fingers through her long hair, trying to smooth and untangle it in one quick motion.

"In the living room. It was the warmest room." Kara gave Taylor a pointed look, her eyebrows arching. "Although maybe that didn't matter, because he's so hot."

"Is he?" Taylor asked, indifferently. She didn't understand all this fuss made over Troy. Yes, he was handsome. But so what? The world was filled with good looking men.

"Seriously hot," Kara drawled.

Taylor rolled her eyes. "Is every woman in this town crazy about him?"

"Every woman with a pulse." Kara winked, and headed back to her bedroom.

Taylor found Troy standing in front of the living room fireplace studying the framed photos on the mantel. She hesitated in the doorway, watching him examine the photos of Kara and her brother growing up.

His dark hair was cropped clean at his nape, showing off his high hard cheekbones and square chin, his strong jaw shadowed with a day old beard. He was wearing a long black wool coat, something you'd probably see in San Francisco's financial district and the tailored wool coat made his shoulders look even bigger, broader, which just emphasized his height.

But then he *was* tall—six two at least—and not the skinny kind of tall, but solid. Muscular. He'd made the huge Escalade feel small and it was probably a very roomy SUV.

"Hi," she said.

He turned to face her. "Sorry to wake everyone up."

As he turned from the mantel, his long black wool coat fell open, exposing his black cashmere sweater, and how it clung to the hard planes of his broad chest.

She'd tried not to stare at his chest in the car.

She had to remind herself not to stare now.

"I'm sorry you had to drive all the way back to Marietta tonight, at this hour." Her voice came out soft, breathless.

THE TYCOON'S KISS

She told herself she was breathless because she wasn't accustomed to greeting men in the Jones' living room. She'd had some double dates with Jane, but none of the men had ever picked her up here. She told herself she was breathless because she was worried about Doug. She couldn't admit she was breathless because he was so...so...different...from any man she'd ever met before.

Nervously, she jammed her hands deeper into the robe pockets, thinking she must look as pretty as a roll of toilet paper in her fuzzy gray robe dotted with fat pink pigs, the robe a Christmas gift from Doug several years ago.

"I didn't want you to panic," he said.

"That was nice of you, because I was, a little bit," she admitted. "I haven't backed up my contacts. Need to." She was babbling. She hated that. But she felt so jumpy. Troy made her self-conscious. And the robe didn't help. She felt silly in the robe. Why hadn't she just put on jeans and a sweatshirt? It would have felt so much safer, and she would have been more confident, than she did greeting him in a pig robe.

Because of course he'd still look urban, and sophisticated. Dashing.

A prince coming to the villager's house with the glass slipper.

Or in this case, a phone.

"I would have waited until morning," Troy said, walking towards her, "but the messages seemed urgent." He handed

39

her the phone. "Hope everything's okay."

His fingertips brushed her palm as he placed the phone in her hand. Taylor blushed, feeling a sharp tingle where his fingers had touched her palm.

This was so absurd. She had to get a grip. She rubbed at the sensitive, tingling spot even as she glanced at the screen of her phone.

Tons of missed calls. Tons of text messages. All from Doug.

"My brother," she said, heart sinking all over again.

"The one in Paradise Valley?"

She nodded. "Do you mind if I send him a message and make sure things are alright?"

"I think that's a good idea. I can always drive you to him if you need a ride."

She didn't bother to explain there were no visits at Hogue Ranch, and no dropping by. The ranch was a halfway house program approved by the state although Taylor wasn't sure how they maintained their status. They weren't doing much for the men there but making them work.

Taylor quickly shot her brother a brief text. *Everything ok?*

*Where have you been?* Doug answered almost immediately.

Taylor typed back. *Had a car accident and lost my phone. But I've got the phone now.*

*You okay?* Doug asked a second later.

*Fine. Car's not so good but that can be fixed.*

*Good. Glad you're safe.*

She drew a deep breath and repeated her first question, dreading his reply. *So are you okay?*

For a long moment there was no response, and then, *I hate it here.*

Taylor bit her lip, a fresh wave of dread washing through her, weighting her limbs, making her heart ache.

He wasn't in the right place. He needed a good therapist, as well as a dedicated doctor who could help with fine tuning Doug's medicine. Not all depression medicine worked equally. Everybody was different. And bodies changed, and brain chemistry changed, and when that happened, you needed to try a new medicine, or a combination of medicines.

Three months she told herself. Three months and he'd be out and she'd get him the right help. She'd make sure he was seen by the best medical professionals she could find.

He deserved it. Just as he deserved a bright, healthy, happy future.

Before she could think of something to say, Doug texted again. *But I'll survive. I'll make it work. I want to get through this so I can come live with you.*

Her eyes burned and her throat swelled closed. For a moment she couldn't breathe, overwhelmed by love. He was such a good person and it broke her heart knowing how much he struggled. Blinking back tears, Taylor texted him back. *Me, too.*

*Will I still see you this weekend?*

*Wouldn't miss it.*

*Nite, Tay.*

*Night, hon.*

She slid her phone into the pocket of her robe, conscious that Troy was watching her, and had been watching her the entire time she'd texted back and forth with Doug. "Everything's fine," she said, voice husky.

"No emergency?" Troy asked.

She managed a small smile, eyes still damp. "Emergency averted."

"That's good."

"Yep." She held her smile and yet on the inside she hurt. She hurt for Doug, and from a purely selfish point of view, she missed him. She hated only being able to see him on weekends, for a couple hours on Sunday. It never seemed as if they had enough time to visit, or just relax and hang out together, playing a game, or watching a show in the living room for guests. It was hard for Doug, too, to have so little contact with family. He was still young. He needed family and support. He needed hugs and laughter and the reminder that he was more than his depression, more than the sum of his parts.

"Thank you," she said to Troy, meaning it. "I know it's a long drive, late at night, in terrible conditions."

"Happy to help." Troy reached into his coat pocket for his car keys. "So how are you going to get to work tomorrow?"

"Kara's dropping me off."

THE TYCOON'S KISS

"Is she also going to help you get a rental car?"

Taylor nodded. "On my lunch."

"Good. Sounds like you have everything in control."

"Kara's good at that."

"I'd imagine."

Taylor walked him to the front door, chewing on the inside of her bottom lip, screwing up her courage to let Troy know she wouldn't be going to the Valentine Ball. *Just say it. Just say it. Just get it over with.*

"Troy," she said, as he reached for the door knob. "About the ball Friday night."

He'd started to turn the knob but he released it and faced her. "Yes?"

He was so tall, so big, and movie star handsome that for a moment her mind went blank. For a moment she just stared at him, dazzled.

And then she blinked, and the moment passed, and she remembered why he was in town, and how the big ball was in just four days.

"I can't go with you," she said quickly, blurting the words before she could change her mind. "And I wanted to let you know now, so you'd have time to find another... date."

Troy didn't immediately speak. His jaw firmed and his dark blue gaze met hers. "Something came up?"

Taylor thought of all the different excuses she could give him—her brother needed her, she had a library conference to attend out of town, her parents would be in town—but she didn't think it was fair to lie to him, especially not after he'd done her two favors.

He'd been quite the gentleman. She owed him the truth.

"I'm not a black-tie formal event kind of girl," she said. "And I'm happy serving on the Wedding Giveaway committee, and selling tickets, but I never wanted to go to the ball. Unfortunately, Jane can be stubborn and doesn't really listen." Taylor's voice dropped, deepening. "I'm sorry if I'm leaving you in the lurch, but honestly, there are so many women who'd probably love to go to the ball with you, and now… one of them can."


TROY DROVE TO the hotel bemused.

The little mouse, his prickly librarian, had just rejected him.

She didn't want to go to the ball, and she definitely didn't want to go with *him*.

Troy wasn't sure how to react. Wasn't sure if he should laugh, or turn his car around and ask her to explain. Why exactly had she told him no?

Because she wasn't a black-tie kind of girl?

Because she didn't want to go to a Valentine Ball?

His brow furrowed. He slowed as he turned into the Graff Hotel parking lot, windshield wipers moving quickly to bat away the falling snow.

He didn't mind that she didn't want to go. He actually

THE TYCOON'S KISS

was relieved. They clearly weren't ever meant to be a couple.

And yet…he was so used to women chasing him, pursuing him, wanting him, that it was a bit of a surprise to meet a woman who didn't want him.

*At all.*

Troy's lips curved as he pulled before the hotel, and handed his keys to the red-cheeked valet attendant.

He'd been impressed by Taylor's resume over the summer. He'd appreciated her experience and knowledge of modern library science, and now he was intrigued.

Why was she so determined not to attend the Valentine Ball with him? Because he had a sneaking suspicion that she would have gone…if he had been someone else.

THE NEXT MORNING an exhausted Taylor stood at the kitchen counter, drinking two cups of coffee and a lightly buttered slice of toast.

It had been next to impossible to fall back asleep last night, after Troy left.

She'd tossed and turned, mashing her pillow this way and that.

Sleep had been elusive. She couldn't turn her brain off. And then when she did finally fall back asleep, she'd dreamed she was wearing this fancy pink prom gown with sparkly bits and little puffed sleeves and she was at the Graff Hotel for the Valentine Ball, only it wasn't really the Graff Hotel's 1914 ballroom, but an 1814 ballroom in London.

Taylor was there with her brother and Jane and feeling very uncomfortable, very much a wallflower, and Jane kept whispering to Taylor about Lord Sheenan, and how handsome he was. Then suddenly somehow Lord Sheenan was asking Taylor to dance and they were twirling and waltzing around the dance floor...

It had all been so vivid, too.

Too vivid.

The ballroom, the gowns, the self-conscious feeling as she stood against a wall, wishing she were home instead of corseted into the ball gown.

And then the waltz, and the way Troy held her, and the feel of him against her.

She'd liked it.

She'd liked it so much she wasn't even sure who had initiated the kiss. Him, or her.

That's when she'd woken up. At the kiss.

The minute she'd woken she wanted to be asleep again, dreaming again. The dream was gone.

She told herself she was glad.

But really, she wasn't.

And so baffled, and grouchy from lack of sleep, she finished the last of her cup, rinsed up her breakfast dishes, and then declined Kara's ride to the library, thinking she needed the walk in the frigid morning air to clear her head.

So bundled up in her winter boots and heavy coat, with her striped scarf wrapped around her neck, Taylor walked

THE TYCOON'S KISS

the ten blocks to the library, down Bramble Lane, the sidewalk mostly shoveled clean and salted.

She had made the right decision about the ball. She was smart to have told him she didn't want to go. He had plenty of time still to find a date. And this way she could stay home Friday night, and curl up with a book.

She'd be so happy reading. She'd be so very content.

She would, she silently insisted. She loved her books. It was the right decision and she was one hundred percent certain that Troy Sheenan would agree.

On break mid-morning at the library, Taylor made calls, filed reports and begged the Bozeman insurance adjustor to go see her car as soon as it was towed to Marietta's body shop, instead of waiting until the next available opening, which was next week.

Then during her lunch, Kara picked up Taylor from in front of the library and drove her to Marietta's only car dealer to pick up a loaner car for the next week.

The loaner car was an older four-wheel drive Jeep, and sketchy at best, but it was a car and it ran, so it was something.

Taylor had hoped to grab a sandwich on her way back to the library but time ran out and she ended up back at work without eating anything. By the time the Tuesday Night Book Club arrived at five thirty for their meeting, Taylor was dragging.

She needed food, and coffee, or just a big cup of coffee.

But there was no time to get anything before the book club discussion began and after an hour and a half Taylor's energy and patience was running low.

She loved her job here in Marietta. She loved this library, too.

Although to be quite honest, right now, Taylor wanted to be anywhere but sequestered in the upstairs conference room with the Tuesday Night Book Group. Her stomach was growling, her head starting to throb from hunger, and she still had the Wedding Giveaway meeting to attend. And Taylor couldn't make it to tonight's wedding committee meeting until she emptied and secured the second floor meeting room for the night.

Emptying the room of this chatty, opinionated group was never easy, but tonight it was starting to appear impossible since three of the founding members of the Tuesday Night Book Club did not like the new chamber director and did not approve of the wedding giveaway in the first place.

"I'm sorry to interrupt," Taylor said, raising her voice to be heard over the fifteen women, and one man, that made up the group. "But we really do need to wrap up. As I mentioned at the beginning of tonight's discussion, I must get to the committee meeting downstairs—"

Maureen continued talking as if Taylor had not spoken.

Taylor pursed her lips, struggling to keep her temper in check. Maureen was one of the ladies that had made Jane's life miserable last November and December and it was

THE TYCOON'S KISS

difficult for Taylor to be in the same room with Maureen. Taylor had little patience for people who had nothing better to do than complain, criticize, and make others miserable.

Unfortunately, it was also Taylor's responsibility to sit in on the various book group meetings and help guide the discussion. It was time to guide this discussion to a closure. She cleared her throat and rose from her chair. "It's time to wrap up," she said firmly. "Sadly, we can't go late tonight—"

"Why not?" Maureen demanded, interrupting Taylor with a question she already knew the answer to. "We always go late."

"We've always been allowed to go as long as we want," Virginia chimed in. Virginia was Maureen's best friend and minion. "I can't remember the last time we had to end at seven thirty."

"You know the Wedding Giveaway committee meeting is about to start downstairs," Taylor said, "and I can't join that meeting until one ends, so let's wrap up, and you can continue at the Java Café if you're still wanting to continue your discussion."

"So how are those tickets selling?" Maureen asked, leaning back in her chair and folded her arms across her stout chest.

"I think the committee said they are at two thirds of their goal," Taylor answered, stacking her book and notepad together and then reaching for the novel. "It would have been nice to sell out, but we've almost one hundred and fifty people attending, and that's fantastic."

"Apparently half of those attending have been given tickets to make the event appear successful," Maureen sniffed. "But I'm not surprised you'd have to do that. Who around here can afford to attend a party that costs two hundred dollars?"

Taylor breathed in, and out, her pleasant smile never once faltering. She'd been a shy little girl, and a quiet, polite, and accommodating teenager. She'd never given her parents any difficulty, and it'd been a shock to all when Doug began having issues in middle school. Her parents didn't know how to cope with a troubled son. They must have made a pact not to deal with it...or him. Their failure to take action had made a lasting impression on Taylor.

"I don't believe that's true, Maureen," she said now. "Yes, big donors and underwriters have been given tickets in exchange for sponsoring the ball, but the committee has sold the majority of the tickets, and it's not two hundred per person, it's two hundred per couple, and that covers dinner, dancing, wine at dinner, and pictures."

Maureen grimaced and stood up, loudly scraping her chair against the hardwood floor. "You'd have to *pay* me to attend a black-tie ball that's being held to launch a wedding contest. Only a Californian would come up with an idea as ridiculous as that."

Taylor opened her mouth to protest, wanting to remind them that the wedding contest was the 100 year anniversary

THE TYCOON'S KISS

of Marietta's 1914 Great Wedding Giveaway, but the group was rising, and gathering their things, and Taylor realized she'd lost that battle. Better to just let them all go.

As the room cleared, Taylor stashed her notepad and book in her leather satchel before checking her phone. A missed call from Jane. Nothing from Doug. Good.

She then went around the room, pushing in chairs, picking up scraps of paper left behind before turning off the lights, locking the door and heading downstairs to the main floor, taking the stairs quickly.

"Off to the wedding committee meeting?" Louise, the children's librarian, asked, passing the foot of the stairs with three children in tow. One of the little girls was Paige Joffee's daughter and the black haired little boy had to be McKenna's son, TJ.

"On my way now," Taylor answered, smiling as TJ chased two little girls around the plant in the lobby corner.

"Apparently Troy Sheenan will be at the meeting, too," Louise said. "Don't know if you've met him, but he's quite something. Marietta's most eligible bachelor and all that."

Taylor arched her eyebrows and pushed her glasses up higher on her nose. Did everyone have a thing for him? "Hadn't heard," she said, trying very hard not to remember her dream last night... and the almost-kiss.

"Jane sent me a text saying she hadn't been able to reach you, but she wanted me to know, which is why I've been hovering a bit in the lobby. I was hoping to give him a hug. I like the Sheenan boys. They've done well for themselves. Very successful young men. Well, all but Trey. Trey's in and out of trouble, but he's not a bad person. He's a sweetheart, he is. He was always my favorite Sheenan." She nodded at the boy who was still chasing the little girls around the potted plant. "See that little guy there? TJ is Trey's boy, and the spitting image of him, too."

Taylor caught a glimpse of TJ's laughing blue eyes and dimples before he chased the little girls in the opposite direction, towards the children's reading room. "No. TJ is McKenna's son."

"And Trey's son."

Taylor frowned. "Trey and McKenna?"

"You didn't know?"

"No."

"They were quite the item. For years." Louise wiggled her fingers, saying goodbye as she raced after the laughing children.

DILLON FOUND TROY in the big Sheenan barn feeding the horses. "You're going to be late," Dillon said, closing the barn door behind him. "Doesn't the meeting start at seven thirty?"

"Yeah."

"It's after seven now."

"I know." Troy brushed feed off his hands, and then wiped his hands on the back of his butt, feeling the stiff

THE TYCOON'S KISS

denim. "I don't want to do this. Dreading this meeting."

"It was your idea," Dillon said.

"The ball wasn't."

"But saving the hotel was."

True, Troy thought, adding water to the trough inside one stall.

*And what a terrible mistake that had been.*

But Troy wouldn't say that out loud, not even to his brother. It'd kill him to admit that restoring the Graff Hotel to its former splendor had the potential to bankrupt him. He should have never invested so much of his own money in one project. A smart investor didn't shell out that much of one's capital. It'd been a mistake to buy the hotel for cash, and even more risky to funnel so much capital into the property. He should have pulled back from the renovation when he realized it was a money pit. But he'd been too proud, too stupid, and too emotionally attached to the project to do the smart thing when he could.

Thank God he was a fighter, and tough. He'd knuckle his way through this battle, because he was nowhere ready to give up on the hotel.

The hotel had only been reopened for six months, after the two and a half year restoration. It'd been a huge job restoring the hotel because it'd been abandoned, boarded up, for over forty years before that. But you wouldn't know it looking at the hotel today. The Graff's grand lobby glowed with rich paneled wood, marble, and gleaming light fixtures,

53

while the grand ballroom and smaller reception rooms sparkled with glittering chandeliers.

And yes, the hotel had virtually zero occupancy since early January, but December had been a good month, with the introduction of festive afternoon tea and company holiday parties on the weekends. But what they needed to do was fill the rooms all the time, because even empty, there were still salaries and bills to pay.

But the hotel was special. She was one of a kind. And while he regretted that restoring her had the power to cost him his company and financial security, he was glad he'd saved her.

Someone had to.

Now he just needed to continue focusing on turning things around, and the hotel staff would. He had a good team here, and everyone in management was committed to making the Graff successful. Troy knew that eventually they could get the hotel into the black. It wasn't impossible.

It was a matter of increasing tourism to Marietta, and getting publicity for the hotel, the kind of publicity that would make the Graff appealing to meeting planners and wedding planners, ensuring that the Graff became the destination of choice for conferences and special events.

"You're in pretty deep, aren't you?" Dillon said, as Troy left the stall and latched the door closed behind him.

"Yeah."

Dillon sat down on a stack of hay bales against the wall,

THE TYCOON'S KISS

extending his legs. "So just how deep?"

Troy reached for his coat hanging on a peg above Dillon's head. "Deep enough that if things go south, I'd be the one living here, working the ranch, leaving you free to return to Austin."

"That'd be a relief for me, but hell for you." Dillon folded his arms across his chest. "You hate the ranch."

Troy's lips compressed. He wasn't going to even dignify that with a response because yes, he did hate the ranch. He hated everything about it, and always had, which is why whenever he came home he stayed in town at a hotel.

"But then, you don't like Marietta, either," Dillon continued, watching Troy button his heavy sheepskin coat. "Which is why none of us can figure out why you'd hitch yourself, and your future, to that damn hotel. You're the smart, successful Sheenan—"

"You and Cormac haven't done too badly for yourselves."

"Because you invested in us."

"I believe in you."

"And the hotel?"

"Not ready to throw in the towel. I've spent ten years investing in startups. I believe can still turn things around."

"But why the Graff in the first place? You're never going to make a profit from the hotel. You might not even earn back the investment."

55

Troy had started walking to the barn door, but he stopped and turned to look back at his brother, and then somehow, just like that, his mother was there. Her ghost. He could feel her at the ranch... in the house, the barn... and her sadness haunted him.

She should have had daughters.

She should have had girls for company. Girls who'd bake with her or sew with her. Girls who'd laugh and giggle and talk to her. Listen to her.

Men weren't good at listening.

He shook his head once, chasing away the past, and the memory of his mother who had loved the Graff. He hadn't restored the hotel for her. That would be idiotic because she was gone. But she had been the one to make him understand that beauty was transformative, and there was value in beautiful things. "Sometimes we do things because we think it's the right thing to do... even when everyone else tells you you're wrong."

Dillon's eyes, narrowed. He studied his older brother a long moment. "Mom would want you to be smart."

"Too late," Troy answered. "Looks like I've inherited her crazy."

Dillon's eyes narrowed another fraction of an inch. "Mom wasn't crazy." He hesitated. "She wasn't happy. That's different from crazy."

Troy said nothing. This was not a subject he liked discussing.

THE TYCOON'S KISS

"And yes, Mom and Dad had problems. From what I gather, no marriage is perfect."

"But not all wives take their lives, do they?" Troy retorted.

Dillon flinched. "It's too late to change the past."

"I just wished I'd done something then."

"How could you? You were a kid. We were all kids."

"I wasn't that young. I knew something was seriously wrong that night."

"I'm sorry you had to be the one to find her. Dad should have checked on her himself."

Troy shook his head. "Let's not go there."

"But you do. Constantly." Dillon's voice hardened. "It's time you let it go. There's no point in torturing yourself, or ruining your future, over something that's in the past."

"Are you talking about Mom or the hotel?"

"Maybe both."

## Chapter Four

TAYLOR WAS RATTLED by Louise's news that Troy would be attending the Wedding Giveaway meeting tonight. She opened the heavy door to the masculine Crawford Room, the private board room off the library's main reading room, wondering why Jane hadn't bothered to tell her that Troy would be coming.

Jane was supposed to be her friend. Her *best* friend in Marietta. And friends did not set friends up, much less with one's gorgeous, popular, ridiculously successful ex.

Most of the committee had already taken a seat at the boardroom table. Taylor's gaze swept the room, seeing all the usual committee members, including McKenna Douglas.

McKenna lifted a hand, gesturing to Taylor.

Taylor moved towards her, seeing McKenna in a new light.

Taylor had known that beautiful McKenna Douglas was a single mom, and a talented photographer specializing in wedding photography, but until tonight she hadn't known

THE TYCOON'S KISS

that Taylor's son's father was Trey Sheenan. McKenna had never said anything, nor had anyone else. Maybe everyone else just knew.

Or maybe folks here didn't think it was important to share. Probably the latter, because no one had told Taylor about the tragedy that took place on Douglas Ranch seventeen years ago. Taylor only found out about the murders by chance, reading through old newspapers and magazines saved in the library's vault.

Taylor, a history buff, had been the one to discover that back in 1914 Marietta had sponsored a big wedding giveaway to draw attention to the re-opening of the Graff Hotel following the 1912 fire. She'd shared the news with Jane, who then came up with the idea of a one hundred year anniversary wedding giveaway, again highlighting the beautifully restored Graff, and all the merchants in town.

Taylor's interest in history and Marietta's 1914 Wedding Giveaway had been a fun surprise, while the discovery of the Douglas home invasion was the opposite.

The horrific crime had sickened Taylor, giving her nightmares for the next few weeks. Worse, the murders had never been solved, and apparently many of the folks in the community thought the crime had to have been someone local...someone who knew the property, the layout of the house, and were familiar to the family, because wouldn't the Douglas' dogs have barked up a storm and alerted the family so they would have had a chance to defend themselves?

Taylor wished she'd never read all the newspaper articles and shook away the grim memories as she joined McKenna. "Hi! How are you tonight?"

"I'm good." McKenna smiled. "Did you see my wild child with Louise?"

"I did. He's found two little girls to chase which is making him very happy."

"Sounds about right. And Louise? She's managing okay?"

"She's great. She loves kids."

"She always has. It's going to be awful when she retires. She's been part of the library since I was born."

"She does love her work," Taylor agreed. "I'm going to miss her, too. She's a sweetheart and has been so helpful since I arrived."

"And Margaret? Has she been as helpful?" McKenna asked, even though she had to be aware that Margaret Houghton, the head librarian, did not believe in new-fangled things like computers and the Internet and had resisted adding e-books to the library's collection.

Taylor grimaced. "Not as helpful, no."

McKenna laughed. "Didn't think so." She hesitated. "Actually, I was hoping I could ask a favor. I need some help tomorrow night."

"You need a sitter?"

"No. Nothing like that." McKenna pushed a long dark auburn strand of hair back from her cheek, securing it behind her ear. "I need a dress for the ball, and I hoped

THE TYCOON'S KISS

you'd go with me to Married in Marietta and give me your opinion. You've seen me. I live in jeans and am useless when it comes to formal attire."

"Of course," Taylor said quickly, pleased and flattered that McKenna wanted to do something with her. "I'd love to."

"You're sure? Dress shopping isn't fun—"

"I would enjoy it. Honestly."

"So you have your dress already?"

"I'm not going to the ball, but I'd love to help you find a dress for Friday night."

"I thought Jane told me you were going." McKenna frowned, shrugged. "I guess I misunderstood. But if you're up for going with me tomorrow night, that's great. I've lined up a sitter so maybe we can make it a girls night out? Shopping and dinner, or shopping and then drinks after?"

"Perfect. Sounds fun."

And it did, Taylor thought, taking a seat on the opposite side of the table, since there were no spots open near McKenna, who was Marietta's golden girl. People genuinely loved her, and were extremely protective of her, which is what made her relationship with Trey Sheenan, Marietta's bad boy, all the more intriguing.

But the meeting was about to start and everyone settled down, pulling out their notebooks and pens.

Paige, from Main Street Diner, went through last meeting's minutes then shared that the Valentine Ball was still shy

61

of its goal with regards to ticket sales, but on the plus side, another twenty had been purchased over the weekend, bringing the expected attendance to 170.

Paige was answering a question about ticket sales when the board room door opened and a tall man in a sheepskin coat and black felt cowboy hat walked in. All conversation died.

He removed his hat, dipped his head. "Sorry I'm late," he said, his voice deep, husky.

*Troy.*

Taylor sat up straighter, her stomach flip flopping wildly.

He looked so... different.

"Welcome," Paige said, smiling at him. "Glad you're here."

He nodded again, his narrowed gaze scanning the room, looking for an available seat.

Taylor hated the way her pulse suddenly danced. There was no reason for her pulse to race. It was embarrassing, actually, to feel anything. So ridiculous that she did.

But she wasn't the only one who seemed affected by Troy. The other women were suddenly sitting taller, and a few were preening. Even calm, practical, unruffled Paige suddenly looked nervous. It'd been several years since the *Copper Mountain Courier* had named Troy Sheenan Marietta's Most Eligible Bachelor, but apparently he hadn't lost any popularity with the ladies since then.

Troy headed to the table. Last night he'd looked like a

city slicker in his cashmere sweater, tailored trousers and black wool coat but tonight he looked imposing in the thick shearling sheepskin coat and scuffed cowboy boots, snowflakes dusting his wide shoulders and long sleeves.

Tonight he wasn't the technology tycoon from California, but a Paradise Valley rancher with Montana running deep in his veins. Tonight he looked like a Sheenan.

Taylor had met two of the other Sheenans in the past month, and both Brock and Dillon were big, dark, ruggedly handsome men. Having changed from his city clothes, Troy looked just as tough. Montana tough.

Taylor hated that she found this new Troy rather appealing. She didn't want to find him appealing. He was Jane's ex. Jane's man. Jane's love. Taylor couldn't forget that, either.

But suddenly Troy's gaze met hers, and held. It was just for a split-second but that split-second was enough to send a rush of blood to her cheeks.

She dropped her gaze, embarrassed, and more than a little flustered. It'd been bad enough telling him she couldn't be his date to the ball, but to spend the next hour in the Crawford Room with him?

She prayed he'd take the empty seat next to Paige. He didn't. He took the chair on her right, and Taylor's heart did a quick staccato as he pulled out the wooden chair and sat down next to her, stretching his legs out beneath the table, boots crossing at the ankle, his denim covered thigh practically touching hers.

"Hello, Taylor," he said under his breath as the meeting resumed.

Her mouth went dry. "Hi," she whispered.

"Get your car situation sorted out?"

She nodded. "Yes. Thank you."

"Good."

The meeting resumed, but Taylor could barely focus on what Paige was saying.

Troy was seriously distracting.

And not just because he was Jane's ex. The man had quite a few attributes.

Like his size. He was a big man... you couldn't ignore him. He filled his chair and all the space around him with shoulders and a big back and hard carved quads.

And a fit man. He had a *body*. And *muscles*. Lots of them. The jaw-dropping, eye-candy sort of body, and now that his heavy coat was off, his snug fitting Henley seemed to stretch over and wrap every sinewy line in his chest and arms, the soft cotton delighting in his dense pecs, flat hard abs, and thick biceps.

Then there was his scent. Which was a lovely, subtle masculine cologne that hinted at spice and something rich and mellow and smooth... vanilla, maybe?

But these attributes were quickly turning into negatives. His scent and warmth and the sheer physicality of the man was proving most distracting.

Taylor fidgeted unhappily, tugging on her notepad,

THE TYCOON'S KISS

drawing it more firmly in front of her. She'd been fine until he arrived. Now she couldn't follow the thread of the discussion, the voices around her a whir of sound, the committee members a blur.

Why had he come tonight?

Meanwhile, various committee members continued updating Troy on various details. There would be flowers everywhere—tulips, roses, lilies, freesias—the most romantic, lush flower arrangements one could imagine, and a DJ and band, and Sage from Copper Mountain Chocolates was in charge of the elaborate dessert buffet, and then some lighting specialists would be bathing the ballroom ceiling in pink lights. It was going to be an incredible ball. Beyond beautiful. And Taylor wasn't going.

And she was glad she wasn't going.

She was.

She really was.


TROY SAT IN the library listening to the committee update its members with the ball details. Everyone was so enthusiastic, and it was the first time Marietta had thrown such an extravagant party so he wasn't surprised ticket sales were down.

After awhile though, the details just became details and he didn't need to hear them all. He zoned out for a bit, studying McKenna's pale face. McKenna was most definitely not good with him here. It hadn't always been the case.

65

They'd once been very close. She was the sister he'd never had. Trey and McKenna had been together off and on since high school, and everyone knew that one day Trey and McKenna would get married. But life kept throwing them curveballs, and it seemed as if McKenna had finally had enough.

He didn't blame her. He couldn't. She'd been a rock in the face of endless chaos and adversity. She deserved a happy-ever-after and she wasn't going to get that with Trey serving time in prison for involuntary manslaughter. True, it was a bar fight he didn't start, but that punch he threw killed a man and the judge came down hard on him, adding some extra time to the mandatory minimum sentence.

Troy sighed. Dad had taken it so hard when Trey was sentenced to five years.

It was then that Dad just seemed to give up.

The family was a mess. The Sheenans had once been a strong, tight-knit family but those days seemed long gone.

Uncomfortable, Trey shifted in the library chair, trying not to glance at his watch, trying not to look at McKenna, trying not to make eye contact with the funny little librarian even though he was very much aware of her.

Last night he'd been surprised by Taylor's refusal to attend the ball with him, but now he was amused. He wasn't accustomed to being rejected. In his world, women chased him and he spent tremendous energy dodging his computer and phone, overwhelmed by the number of women texting

THE TYCOON'S KISS

and calling, instant messaging and sending flirty snapchats. He appreciated a beautiful woman. He admired a smart, beautiful woman. But he wasn't comfortable being chased. He didn't like feeling hunted.

Back in school he'd been popular. The Sheenan brothers were good looking boys. None of them had ever lacked for girls, or dates. But once he'd made his fortune, women weren't just interested in him, they were interested in his lifestyle.

Maybe that's why he'd chosen to sit next to Taylor in tonight's meeting. She didn't eye him as if he were a tasty steak, or a Thanksgiving feast.

She looked at him with indifference, maybe even disdain. But if instead of being insulted, it made him smile. It also made him a little curious. Why did Miss Taylor Harris disapprove of him? Why did she have a problem with him?

It wasn't a challenge, he thought. Or was it?

Because he suddenly wanted to prove her wrong.

A man liked a challenge. A man liked the chase. Provided he was doing the chasing.

So Troy stopped listening to the committee, he gave up trying to keep track of all the details…. no longer caring to remember what kind of flowers or lighting or chocolate desserts there would be.

Instead he studied Taylor who sat with her legs crossed just above the knee, taking copious notes in her notebook, her pink lips pursed, her brow furrowed in concentration.

She looked so studious and focused with her glasses, cardigan sweater, and long gleaming ponytail. He'd always had such a thing for smart girls. Book girls. His sophomore year of high school he'd spent all his free time in this library, making out with Lani Murphy in any dark corner they could find.

They'd study, kiss, study, kiss.

It had been the best academic year of his life.

Sure, his grades hadn't been so hot but he'd felt like a man, and she'd felt well… amazing.

He tried not to smile as he pictured Taylor back in high school. He was quite sure she'd looked the same. Same ponytail, same glasses, same smart, studious expression.

He wondered if she'd ever spent a high school afternoon making out in the library. Somehow from her starchy expression, he suspected not. She struck him as the kind of girl who believed libraries were about books. Silly girl. He'd love to teach her what dark shadowy corners in libraries were really for.

As if aware of his scrutiny, Taylor turned her head and stared back at him, giving him a significant, no nonsense look that he thought was sexy as hell.

Until now he'd thought her eyes were brown, a simple chocolate brown, but now he saw they were a hazel green with bits of light blue. Or was it silver?

With her brows arching, dark elegant wings behind the masculine frames, and her hazel eyes snapping fire, he

THE TYCOON'S KISS

thought she'd never looked quite so bright and beautiful.

If only she understood that she looked very appealing annoyed.

Quite kissable with her pink lips pursed.

"*What?*" she mouthed at him.

"What, *what?*" he whispered back.

Her nostrils flared as she exhaled hard. "You're staring."

Heads were turning. Everyone seemed to be looking at them now but McKenna, who was looking away.

Troy leaned closer to Taylor. He spoke under his breath. "I like your glasses."

For a moment Taylor just looked at him, her expression incredulous, and then she leaned very close to him, so close he could smell a hint of citrus and orange blossom. Shampoo or fragrance, he didn't know which.

"They're not a fashion statement," she said quietly, tersely. "I need them to see. Now *sshh*. We're interrupting the meeting."

WHY DID SHE say that?

The moment the words left her mouth, Taylor wanted to die of mortification. *Sssh. We're interrupting the meeting.* She sounded like such a fuddy-duddy. Like the crabbiest old woman alive.

Like Margaret Houghton, Marietta's head librarian.

But Taylor wasn't Margaret, nor was she crabby. Taylor was an optimist. And a closet romantic. But even optimists and closet romantics had to know when they were out-classed.

Troy wasn't in her class, or her league, or anything at all that she could be part of.

She and Troy might as well exist on different planets and spheres.

She wasn't a big city girl. She didn't like social functions. She loved disappearing into bed with a wonderful story.

And yes, one day she hoped to find true love... that wasn't in a romance novel... and she was sure, one day, she'd find Mr. Right, and when she did, he would make sense to her, and suit her, and reflect her morals and values.

He'd be a simple man, too. A homebody. A man who loved books and... and....

Taylor frowned.

What else would he love?

Sports? Hiking? Skiing? Mountain climbing?

Her frown deepened.

She didn't do any of those things. But she did like movies, and she enjoyed some good quality television programs.

She loved B&Bs and scenic drives. She loved visiting historical spots, too, and hoped one day to visit all the national parks in the States.

Surely there was a man out there who'd like her, and want to do those things with her, too.

Surely.

And when she did find him, she'd know he was right.

THE TYCOON'S KISS

He'd look right. He'd feel right. He'd be right.

TROY HAD BEEN waiting for the committee meeting to come to an end so he could speak to McKenna. He wanted to come see TJ one night this week while he was home but the moment the meeting did end, McKenna was on her feet and bolting out the door.

Troy tried to follow but Paige stopped him and asked a question about the suite being donated to the Great Wedding Giveaway for the bridal couple, and by the time he'd answered her question and made it into the hallway, McKenna and TJ were long gone.

He was still standing there, when Taylor exited the boardroom and locked the door on the now empty room. "Everything okay?" she asked him, even as Louise emerged from the back of the library, turning off lights as she went.

"Yes," he said, but he was frustrated. He loved McKenna. Loved TJ. He didn't want to lose them and he was beginning to worry that maybe he already had.

"Were you hoping to catch McKenna?" Taylor asked.

He nodded.

Louise glanced from Troy to Taylor, said goodnight, and then headed out, leaving Troy and Taylor in the hall.

"I'll walk you out," he said. "Make sure you get to your car safely."

"I have a few things to do first," Taylor said. "So don't wait. I'll be fine. Marietta's safe."

"I'm not going to leave until you're safely at your car," he answered firmly.

So he waited while she double-checked that the computers were powered down and the lights were off in the restrooms, and just when she was ready to go, she remembered the reading she'd needed to do at home, and returned to the staff room to grab a stack of industry magazines.

"Are you going to read all that tonight?" he asked, nodding at the stack she'd bundled against her chest.

"I'll skim everything. It's good to stay up on industry news."

His lips curved and it was all he could do to not comment on what must be a wildly exciting industry. There was no point in baiting her. She took her job very seriously and he had to admire her commitment.

They exited the front door and Taylor locked the door and set the alarm. Her teeth were chattering as she punched in the alarm code. "It's cold," she said, slipping her glove on.

"It's been a long winter for most of the country," he agreed.

"I take it you all haven't been suffering too much in California?" she asked, shooting him a wry look.

"No. It's been a really mild winter on the West. We could use some good storms in California. Need the rain. We've been in a drought for quite some time."

"Why do you like California?"

"Besides the balmy winters?" he asked, flashing her a

smile. "It's just where the opportunity is for me. I like cities and innovation, and Silicon Valley is the home for many startups and technology, so it's where I am, too."

They were heading down the stairs for the parking lot and he saw Taylor glance at him, another one of her quick, shrewd glances. "You don't miss Montana?"

There was no easy way to answer a question like that, he thought. His family situation made coming home complicated, if not downright uncomfortable. It was easier when his dad wasn't ill. Easier to keep all the emotions and memories locked away. "Marietta will always be home, but my head is clearer in California. I function better there. Not so many ties and entanglements." He grimaced, and shook his head. "I suppose that sounds ridiculous—"

"No," she interrupted, bundling her arms tighter across her chest. "I'm quite ambivalent to Hopeville. I don't find it easy or comfortable going home, so I appreciate your honesty. It's reassuring."

"You don't go home often then?"

"No."

"You don't get along with your folks?"

"I get along fine with them, or at least, I used to until I took my brother under my wing. They didn't appreciate my interference, and it has strained the relationship—which is quite an understatement—but I did what I had to. They were neglectful and didn't treat him the way he deserved."

"You're very protective of him."

"I have to be. What's happened isn't his fault. None of it is his fault."

"So you're not just his big sister, but his surrogate mom now."

She nodded once and squared her shoulders. "You could say that."

Looking down at her small face with the resolute press of pink lips, he felt a funny little pang. She really wasn't like the other women he knew. He was glad. He liked her honesty. He was glad she wasn't trying to impress him. "Would you want to grab a quick bite with me at Main Street Diner? I think they're open for another hour."

She made a face. "It's late."

"I know you haven't eaten. Louise said you had no chance to grab anything before all of tonight's meetings."

"I can eat when I go home."

"Louise said you'd just have soup."

"And I would, it's true."

"She thinks you need some proper meals."

Taylor's jaw firmed and yet her eyes were smiling. "Louise shouldn't be sharing my personal life with you."

"I've known her since I was just a little kid and she has a good heart. I respect her, and appreciate that she's looking out for you."

"She is one of my favorite people in Marietta, and she is right. I could use some real food. Besides," she added, smiling wider, suddenly sounding mischievous. "It's Tuesday."

"This is good because…?"

"Tuesday means homemade beef barley soup at the diner."

"Soup?" he laughed.

She grinned. "What can I say? I like soup. But don't worry, I'll order a salad, too."

## Chapter Five

THEY CUT THROUGH Crawford Park, towards the courthouse before crossing Front Street for the Main Street Diner.

Marietta had been so pretty with all the Christmas lights and decorations up. Now it just looked empty and a little dirty with white and gray snow heaped in the gutter and on all the street corners.

Taylor was glad to reach the diner to get out of the biting wind. Fortunately, at almost nine, the restaurant was virtually empty. The waitress told them they could sit anywhere and Troy left the choice to Taylor.

Taylor selected one of the big leather booths along the brick wall and once seated, she peeled off her coat and scarf and hat, piling them next to her. Suddenly she thought of McKenna, and how McKenna had avoided looking at Troy, and how Troy had gone after McKenna but she'd left without speaking to him.

"I didn't realize until tonight that your brother Trey was

the father of McKenna's son," Taylor said.

Troy gave her a wary glance. "You and McKenna aren't close?"

"No, but I like her. I've always wanted to get to know her better, and tomorrow night we're supposed to go look at dresses. Well, she's trying on gowns. McKenna wants me there for moral support and maybe my advice."

"Have you met Lawrence, her fiancé?"

"Briefly, but I do see him around. His office is on Main Street. He and McKenna both work in the same building, down by the Mercantile."

"I don't know him."

"He seems nice, and very devoted to McKenna. He's watched TJ a couple times when McKenna attends the Wedding Giveaway committee meetings. He and TJ will hang out in the children's book section while we meet in the Crawford Room."

"So McKenna is excited about the wedding?"

"I would think so. I imagine I'll learn some details tomorrow night."

"I hope she'll be happy," he said, picking up the menu. He studied it for a minute before setting it aside. "She deserves to be happy. McKenna is amazing, and a great mom to TJ."

Taylor lifted a brow. "But..?"

His big shoulders shifted. "But nothing. Trey had the best girl—the best thing—and he screwed it up."

"Did you love McKenna, too?"

"Of course I love her. Everybody loves McKenna. She's just... that... special, but if you're asking if I was in love with her, that's a no. She was always Trey's girl. Always. I would never, ever go there. Trey's my twin."

"Can't imagine two of you," Taylor answered. "Does Trey really look just like you?"

"We're identical, but we've never dressed alike, or played the twins card. We've always been so different. Trey was quite a bit older than McKenna so they only flirted in high school, and began dating once McKenna had graduated from Marietta High. McKenna's brothers, Rory and Quinn, did not want their sister dating Trey. She was this sweet, good girl and he was the terrible, bad boy but they clicked."

"Opposites attract," Taylor said.

He nodded. "She made him better and he made her laugh, and when it was good between them, it was very good, but when it was bad, it was hell. I don't know how many times they broke off, only to get back together before another bruising break up. They were broken up— apparently for good—when McKenna discovered she was pregnant. It took her a long time to take him back, and then it was magic. Trey proposed, she'd accepted, and they were planning a wedding when Trey got in trouble. Now he's gone for a couple years."

"He got in a bar fight?"

"Some guy was getting rough with his girl over at the

Wolf Den and Trey got involved, threw a punch, and the other guy hit his head on a table as he fell. He later died. Trey was arrested, and sentenced to three to five years for involuntary manslaughter."

Taylor didn't know what to say.

Troy shrugged. "It's bad."

"I'm sorry."

"I am, too." Troy lifted a hand, flagged the waitress down. "It's late. We should probably order."

They steered away from personal topics while they ate, discussing the ball for a bit, and then the Great Wedding Giveaway, before circling back to Taylor's new job at the library.

"I love my job," she said, answering Troy's question. "And I love the building itself. The library has such a great history, built in the 1880's as the third public building constructed during Marietta's short-lived copper boom, and it's handsome, with all those tall windows, the high ceilings, the marble foyer and staircase with hardwood floors on the first and second floors—" She took a breath. "But as it is now, it just feels old. I don't know if you've noticed, but the library has a dusty, musty feel. And yet it's clean. The problem is just that it's never been updated. Even the glass display cabinets are filled with displays decades old."

Troy smiled, enjoying how animated she'd become while talking about the library. She was passionate about her work and dedicated, too. The hiring committee had made the right decision, recommending her for the job. "What would you do with the library, if you could?"

"Besides change those ancient displays?" she asked, smiling crookedly. "Well, for one, I'd make the library a true community center. I'd overhaul the electrical—new lights and outlets throughout so people could bring their laptops and study there. I also think that the smaller conference room on the second floor would be perfect for a little café or espresso stand."

"Espresso at the library?"

Taylor nodded. "It's happening at libraries, and can't you just see how good it would be for moms? They could grab a coffee and have a little visit or read a magazine while their kids went to story time with Louise. I think Marietta teens and local college students would enjoy a coffee or snack while studying. But of course, Margaret, won't hear of us changing a single thing, library, whether it's one of her faded but 'culturally relevant' display cases, or those hollow antiquated private rooms on the second floor that go unused, unless one of the book groups meet in them."

"This is how it all starts, you know."

"What does?"

"Change. You have an idea, and you get excited and throw your weight behind it and before you know it, you're in really deep and everyone else is wondering what the hell happened."

"Is that what happened with you and your hotel?"

"Pretty much."

"But isn't that good? Look what you've given back to Marietta."

"Not everyone here is happy about it. Not everyone likes change, even if it's beneficial."

"Why?"

"Because some people are afraid of change. They're afraid it means they might have to grow and change, and that could be hard work."

"Well, I'm not asking anyone to change. I just want to improve the library. I'd like to make the library a thriving community center. Why not let that gorgeous old building become the heart of the community? A library is more than books and quiet spaces. A library should inspire, enrich, and support both individual patrons and the community—" she broke off and bit into her lower lip. "Maybe I am asking for some change."

He smiled, liking her more and more, as well as impressed by her spirit. Who would have thought that the pretty new librarian had such fire? "Good. And don't ever apologize for wanting to do something here, or anywhere. We need people with passion and vision. I admire your enthusiasm. But can I offer you one piece of advice?"

"Yes."

"Don't fall in love with beautiful historic buildings in small towns."

"No?"

"*No*. It's a maddening love, and very expensive."

She sat back in the booth, expression thoughtful. "I've wondered about that."

"I'm sure everyone has."

"So why did you do it?"

"The hotel is…." his voice drifted off and he stared off, picturing it as it was when he bought it—the boarded up windows, the ratty stained carpet covering the marble lobby, the holes in the walls and then that ballroom, the grand ballroom with its soaring ceiling and gilt trim, and the old reading room with its rich walnut paneling. He could feel the history in the abandoned building, set for demolition. He could picture the dances and the blushing brides and how stately even the old coatroom outside the ballroom must have been.

And he'd bought it on the spot.

For cash.

Because no one would loan him money for that eye sore. No one could see how it'd ever be restored and put back on the market without bleeding the investors dry.

And the hotel was bleeding him dry, but it was also beautiful now. A landmark. A Montana treasure. And he did feel good about that. He had done something right. Maybe not everyone would agree, or understand, but he remembered going to the Graff with his mother and brothers when he was young, just before it had closed, to see the Christmas tree in the big lobby, and have hot chocolate in the restaurant.

THE TYCOON'S KISS

They'd all dressed up, his mom and her four boys—Dillon wasn't born yet—and Trey had been bored but Troy had been enthralled.

When he grew up, he'd live like this.

When he grew up, he'd give his mother a beautiful palace, just like this.

Troy suddenly became aware that Taylor was looking at him, and waiting, patiently for him to finish.

He looked into her face, and saw her eyes and her interest and she was interested in hearing what he had to say. Not because he was a Sheenan. Not because he was rich. But interested in what he thought, and felt.

What he knew.

Who he was.

Something inside him shifted. He felt some of the tension he'd been carrying around with him ease. He smiled wryly. "The hotel needed to be saved. It's part of me, and Marietta, and it was supposed to be demolished. The building had been condemned, and I couldn't let it happen. So I didn't."

Her gaze held his, her expression intent. "Do you regret saving it?"

"No."

"Even if it… hurts you… financially?"

"Jane's been talking."

Taylor pursed her lips. She appeared to choose her words carefully. "The whole town's been talking."

"Not surprised. But I have good instincts. I think it's going to be alright."

"You're sure?"

"Yes. Because even if I have to sell it at some point, and even if I take a loss, I've still won. I've given something back to my hometown. I've created something that my children and grandchildren can enjoy. And that makes it all worth it."

TAYLOR LOOKED DOWN at her plate, and blinked, fighting the most ridiculous urge to cry. Her eyes had burned and turned gritty as he'd talked about creating something for his children and grandchildren. She understood his love for old buildings and the past. She'd always been fascinated by old black and white photographs of Montana's past. If she looked hard enough into one of those photographs she could imagine herself there...

"I wish I could have seen the Graff before you restored it," she said. "But maybe it's good that I didn't. It would have made me sad."

"She was too beautiful to be neglected like that," he agreed.

For a long moment Taylor said nothing, her emotions turbulent, her thoughts whirling. She shouldn't say what she was so tempted to say. She shouldn't even be feeling what she'd been feeling all night.

She should get her purse and coat and go home right now.

THE TYCOON'S KISS

Right now without saying a single thing about the ball. Or maybe, possibly going to the ball with him.

She couldn't. She'd already told him no. She'd made up her mind. Taylor wasn't flighty. At least, she'd never been flighty before…

Taylor swallowed hard and reached for her leather satchel. She needed to leave before she said something she might regret.

And yet her heart raced. She couldn't remember when she last felt so torn.

"I'm glad we did this," she said. "It was nice. Thank you."

"I enjoyed it, too."

She pulled the satchel onto her lap, and reached for her wallet.

He saw her open the wallet and shook his head. "I've got this."

"It's not a date," she answered.

He smiled. "I know. But I can write it off. It's probably harder for you."

"That's true. There is no budget at the library for meals or entertainment. Not even for technology."

Troy placed several twenties on the table. "Which will change when Margaret's gone in June."

"I hope so." Taylor glanced from the bills to Troy's chest, where the snug Henley hit, just beneath his collarbone, exposing taut tone muscle and golden skin. He was

85

obviously able to get some sun in California. Lucky man.

And then suddenly before she even knew she'd committed to the idea, she blurted, "Troy, I was thinking about the ball."

"I'm not surprised. You've been working very hard on the committee."

"I meant. I was thinking about…" Her voice faded. Her courage faded. She couldn't do it. Couldn't put herself back out there. It was too embarrassing. And she shouldn't be going to the ball. She'd already told both Jane and Troy that. To change her mind now showed lack of stability and judgment. Besides, he might have already found a date.

That stopped her cold.

She studied him, taking in his straight nose, the high cheekbones and his firm mobile mouth quirking in a half-smile. He was so masculine and relaxed… so confident.

She was not.

She'd never had his self-assurance. "Were you able to find a date?" she asked, thinking it was one thing to talk books and technology and historical renovation with him. It was another to discuss… dates. "I was certain you would. Just wanted to be sure. I hate to think I've left you in the lurch."

The corners of his lips curved higher. "Haven't found another date yet, no."

Her heart fell. "I'm sorry."

"It's my fault. I haven't asked anyone else."

THE TYCOON'S KISS

"Why not?"

"I wanted to go with you."

Her pulse jumped. "I see."

"You do?"

"Yes."

But she didn't, and Taylor almost kicked herself under the table for saying things she didn't mean, because she didn't see. She didn't understand. She didn't understand why Troy would want to go to the ball with her. But somehow, between leaving the library and finishing her apple pie *a la mode*, she wanted to go to the ball with Troy.

As friends, of course, she added hurriedly.

But she did want to go. She wanted to be part of the historic night and see the ballroom all lit up with pink lights and taste the chocolates and sip champagne...

And it would be fun to go, with him, provided it wasn't romantic. Provided they were... just friends.

Taylor squeezed her satchel, thinking she was most definitely in over her head and yet she was going to press on, and just do this. Of course he could reject her. She fully expected a rejection any moment. "Troy, I was thinking—" her voice quavered, broke, courage once again stalling. She stared across the table at him, no longer certain of anything.

TROY HEARD TAYLOR'S voice quaver and crack before she went silent. He watched the color storm her cheeks, and then saw her bite down into her lower lip, teeth ruthless and intent.

He was quite interested in what she'd have to say next. "Yes?" he prompted.

"Maybe I could go to the ball… with you," she rushed and stumbled through the words, before pausing to meet his gaze, her chin lifting fractionally, almost defiantly, "if we went as just… friends."

"Friends," he repeated, looking at her, and trying not to obsess over the fact that her glasses were slipping down the length of her small, straight nose and he itched to lean forward and push them back up. Not because the glasses annoyed him on the tip of her nose—they didn't—he found it quite endearing. She looked like a very young and very pretty librarian. He'd always had a thing for smart girls, book girls and here was the epitome of a smart, book girl before him.

A single, smart book girl. Who also happened to be quite level-headed, and sweet.

Well, her soft pink lips looked quite sweet. He found the bow shape of her lips incredibly appealing. They were the lips of a pin-up, not a prim librarian, and Troy wondered if she'd kiss like a pin-up, or a prim librarian. He was tempted to kiss her now just to find out.

It probably wouldn't do.

It might just scare her off.

As it was, she wanted to be… *friends.*

"I would hope we're friends," he said pleasantly, lazily.

THE TYCOON'S KISS

"Yes, but only *friends*," she said, emphasizing the friends part yet again. She sat up taller, shoulders squared. "I was thinking I might enjoy the ball if it were purely platonic between us."

She *might* enjoy the ball... if it was purely platonic between them.

His lips twitched.

But she wasn't done yet.

"Troy, you seem like a nice man, but here's my quandary—"

"Yes. What is your quandary?" he asked.

She pushed up her glasses, and sighed. "You are Jane's ex and I appreciate that there's nothing between you now, but it makes me uncomfortable, knowing that you were together and that she continues to have... some feelings... for you, so it's best that we be just friends. Nothing romantic. Which is why, if you still need a date for the ball, I'm happy to be that date, but I just want to be sure we're on the same page, about... romance... and things."

"If Jane were not in the picture, would your feelings be different?" he asked, amused.

Taylor hesitated, frowned, and then tugged uneasily on her ear lobe. "I can't say. I don't know. No... I don't think so. I think I'd still only want to be friends with you. I don't think a romantic relationship would work between us."

She was so earnest that Troy bit down on the inside of his cheek to keep from laughing out loud. Thank goodness he'd grown up in a family of boys and had developed a healthy sense of self-esteem. He might have found her rejection bruising otherwise.

It took him a moment to gather his thoughts.

"What is it about me you don't like?" he asked.

"It's not personal—" Taylor broke off, frowned, dragged her coffee cup and saucer closer to the edge of the table. "Well, maybe it is. And that's not fair of me, but the fact that you and Jane have history, and the fact that Jane continues—" she broke off again, her cheeks turning pink. Her gaze fell to the table, her long black lashes dropping to hide her eyes. She pushed the saucer again. "She's my friend, my good friend, and I don't want to create problems for you, or her, or me."

"Most admirable," he said, meaning it, finding everything about Taylor interesting and refreshing. "But you do know that Jane and I were friends before we dated, and we dated briefly as an experiment—an experiment that didn't work out—but we managed to preserve and protect our relationship, so that we continue to be good friends today."

"How long were you… together?"

"I don't know that you could say we were ever truly together."

"Jane was in love with you!"

He frowned. "I know she says that—"

"You doubt her feelings?"

Troy stifled a sigh. He shouldn't have ever gone down

this path. "No, I don't," he said firmly. "But Jane and I only dated for a couple weeks. Two and a half. Three. For a total of five dates. I knew it wasn't right on date one, but I liked Jane so much. I liked her fire and ambition. She's a great girl, and a marketing genius. It was easy to spend time with her. But at the end of the day, I didn't have... romantic... feelings for her."

Taylor stared at him from across the table, her eyes wide, expression somber. "Then you shouldn't have slept with her."

Troy's jaw dropped. "*What?*"

"You should never sleep with a woman you don't have feelings for." Taylor's soft full lips pressed into a hard, uncompromising line. "Women fall in love through making love. It's a bonding thing for us. Hormones and chemicals and—"

"We never slept together," he interrupted, irritated, not just by the direction their conversation had taken, but by Taylor's low opinion of him. "We never had sex. Jane and I had too much history to just jump into bed together."

For a moment Taylor said nothing, gazing at him intently from behind her big glasses.

For the first time since they'd sat down she seemed to have nothing to say.

Good.

He was fed up with this conversation, as well as having to defend himself. He didn't even know why he felt compelled to defend himself to a little mouse. Except for some ridiculous reason he wanted her to understand how the relationship with Jane had been. Not how Jane had wanted it to be.

"Not everybody clicks," he said crisply, battling his impatience and annoyance. "Not every man and woman belongs together."

He saw a flicker in her wide green-brown eyes and a tiny pulse begin to dance at the base of her throat and he wished to God he could read Taylor's mind right now and know what she was thinking. Feeling.

Did she truly have no feelings for him at all?

Or was she that protective of Jane?

Or was she simply... scared... that they were so different?

"A relationship can't go the distance without friendship and mutual respect," he said, "but there must also be chemistry."

"Chemistry," she repeated, before chewing on the inside of her soft lower lip.

He eyed the lip, seeing how her white teeth bit down into the pink plumpness and he wished it was his mouth on hers.

If only to know if they had chemistry.

It would be such a relief if there wasn't anything between them. It would be the best thing for both of them if he kissed her and he felt nothing... absolutely nothing.

He should kiss her and find out.

Kiss her and be done with this foolishness.

They weren't meant for each other. Troy didn't do long distance relationships. Troy didn't ever intend to live in Montana again.

"You didn't have chemistry with Jane?" Taylor asked quietly.

"No."

She fidgeted with the small ceramic saucer. "How did you know?"

"Because when I kissed her I felt…" He shook his head, not wanting to go there, not wanting to expose Jane but he felt caught, trapped. The villain and blackheart.

"Yes?" Taylor prompted, her voice but a whisper.

"Like her cousin or brother." He hated saying all of this aloud. He wanted to protect Jane then, and now. "She's smart and witty and perfect… for someone else, that isn't me."

He drew a deep breath, feeling awful. He'd disliked breaking the news to Jane eighteen months ago, and didn't enjoy revisiting the topic now. "I ended it quickly with her. Perhaps that was the most hurtful part. We had a great date the Saturday night before, and she was expecting another great date, but instead over dinner I told her that although I cared for her, it wasn't going to work. Would it have been easier by text or email or voice mail? Yes. But it wouldn't have been fair to her. I don't lead women on. It's never been my style."

For a long moment Taylor studied him, her fine arched brows pulled in concentration. "So you could just be friends with me?"

"Absolutely."

He saw relief in her eyes. And then he ruined it all by adding, "As long as I didn't physically desire you."

Her brows shot up. Her shoulders squared. "You *wouldn't* desire me."

"No?"

"*No.* I'm not your type, and you're not my type—"

"What is your type?"

She gestured a hand in his general direction. "None of this."

He should be insulted. Instead he nearly choked on smothered laughter. "Why not?"

"Because we're total opposites. We're oil and water. We're salt and pepper—"

"And yet all those things go so well together."

She glared at him even as her cheeks glowed pink, a dark luscious pink that made her eyes shine and her lips look positively edible. "We won't go together. We won't... click."

"How can you be so sure?"

"I can feel it."

And yet her eyes were very bright and that little pulse at the base of her throat was beating wildly. Erratically. She was very aware of him, and very much engaged in the moment.

THE TYCOON'S KISS

And Taylor might not admit it, might not even know it, but she was as curious about him as he was about her.

And he was very curious about her right now. About her mouth and her taste and her smell...

"Perhaps you'd feel better putting it to the test?" he drawled, smiling inwardly as her eyes sparked and her teeth came down on the bottom lip again. "That way you can rest," he said, his blood hot in his veins, his body heavy, thick. "Relax," he added, "reassured that you are right, and that there is... *nothing*... here."

Silence followed.

The silence crackled and burned.

She licked the seam of her lips as if her mouth was suddenly too dry.

Just like that, he hardened. At thirty-six Troy Sheenan didn't walk around with erections, or get spontaneous erections. He wasn't aroused by merely pretty faces, either. Not anymore. Because he craved more from a woman than lips and breasts and a firm butt.

He needed more. He needed his mind engaged and his senses engaged. Like they were now.

His pulse drummed harder, faster.

She wondered if there was chemistry.

He'd bet a thousand dollars—no, *five* thousand dollars—there was serious chemistry here, and she was either too innocent, or too inexperienced to recognize it. But this tension, this heat, this frustrating and yet wonderful anticipation *was* chemistry.

"Lean forward," he said.

"*What?*"

"I'm going to kiss you and see if I feel anything. If I don't, then I can safely promise you that if you went to the ball with me, it'd just be as platonic friends."

"But if you do?" she whispered, brows knitting.

"Then I'd probably have a difficult time just viewing you in a platonic light."

"So we couldn't go to the ball."

"Or we could, and we'd both have a lot of fun, knowing that we're attending a very special event for Marietta, something that might not ever happen again. We'd dine and dance, and sip champagne, and I can promise you that there would be no other woman in the ballroom that I'd rather be with, than you."

Taylor stared at him and swallowed hard.

Tired of talking, fed up with thinking and waiting, Troy leaned across the table, captured her chin in his hand, and covered her mouth with his.

# Chapter Six

HIS MOUTH FELT firm and cool against hers and yet somehow the pressure of his lips against hers, made her skin burn and her lips tingle.

Hot, electric darts of sensation raced through her, making her ache.

Making her want more.

Her lips parted beneath his and she felt the tip of his tongue on the inside of her lip and she nearly whimpered at the pleasure of it.

He ended the kiss, stroked his thumb across her cheek and then sat back and regarded her from beneath lowered lashes.

"Well?" Taylor whispered, amazed that a kiss could feel so good.

"I think we can be friends."

Her heart fell. He felt no chemistry with her, and it's what she wanted. At least, it's what she told herself she wanted. But hadn't she also told him the very same thing?

Taylor pressed her lips together, fighting the sudden urge to cry. "Good," she said huskily. "That's great news."

"So you think you can manage the ball?"

Her eyes felt hot and gritty and she swallowed hard. "Should I just meet you there?"

"You don't want me to pick you up?"

"Well, if we're just friends, it seems silly to make you leave your own hotel to come get me."

"I don't mind."

"I know you don't. You're quite nice about things like that, and I still appreciate you taking the time to return my phone to me last night."

"Friends do nice things for each other."

She struggled to smile but couldn't. Her eyes burned and her throat ached and she wanted to climb into her bed and pull her covers up over her head and cry.

And she didn't even know why she wanted to cry. It's not as if she liked him. It's not as if she had any feelings for him, either...

"So I'll pick you up," he said after a moment. "How does five forty-five sound?"

"Good," she said.

"Great. It's a date."


TROY WALKED TAYLOR back to the library parking lot. He waited until she'd safely left before he started his SUV.

He'd eaten dinner but he needed a drink.

THE TYCOON'S KISS

He was staying at the Graff tonight, and he could easily get a drink there. It'd be convenient to pull up to the hotel, have valet take the car, and be done with it. He'd get served fast in the bar, too, as the staff at the hotel knew him and jumped to please him, but Troy wasn't comfortable with all the jumping and scraping. The constant display of deference put him on edge. For God's sake, this was Marietta, Montana and he wasn't a Rockefeller but a Sheenan.

One didn't bow and scrape to a Sheenan. Sheenans got into scrapes. Sheenans were tough and practical. Sure, Troy had made some money in the fifteen years since he finished college, good money, money didn't make a man, and money certainly didn't define him.

Troy drove down Main Street to Grey's Saloon.

No one at Grey's bowed and scraped. Grey didn't tolerate airs. The only one at Grey's Saloon with attitude was Grey himself, the surly bastard.

Troy stepped from his SUV, pocketed his keys, entered the corner building, and took a seat at the bar. Tonight it was Reese behind the counter and Reese poured Troy a shot of whiskey, neat, before giving Troy space. Good man.

Troy nursed the whiskey for a bit, welcoming the space and quiet. After a bit, Reese returned and they talked the way men liked to talk, about not much of anything, which was the best sort of conversation because it was never too personal and, therefore, never too uncomfortable. Men didn't need to share their feelings, not like women.

"Another one?" Reese asked, approaching Troy and gesturing to his empty tumbler.

Troy nodded and slid the glass across the counter.

Taylor Harris kissed like a pin up. Her lips were soft and sweet but she kissed with heat.

There'd been serious heat in that kiss. Serious chemistry, too.

Troy hardened again, remembering.

"You're in town for the ball," Reese said as he placed the fresh whiskey in front of Troy.

"Yeah."

"Who are you taking?"

Troy shifted. "Taylor Harris."

Reese frowned. "Do I know her?"

"She's the new librarian."

"The librarian?" Reese shot him an amused glance. "Not your usual type."

Troy chose not to dignify the remark. He took a long drink from his glass. The whiskey burned going down, a good kind of burn. "So are you going Friday night?" he asked Reese.

"To the ball?" Reese shook his head. "Not my thing."

"Apparently it's not a lot of folks' thing." Troy grimaced. "Seemed like a good idea back in the fall, but I've been away from Montana a long time. I'd forgotten that folks here aren't into fancy dress balls."

"Especially in the dead of winter."

"Winter's harsh this year."

"Winter is harsh here every year." Reese leaned against the counter behind him. "I guess it's easy to forget the twenty below zero wind chill when you don't even need a coat in February in San Francisco."

"Oh, you need a coat in San Francisco. But just a thin one," Troy retorted. He raised his glass. "To all the idealistic bastards in the world with more balls than brains."

"The world needs idealistic bastards to balance out the assholes and realists."

"Which one are you?"

Reese smiled darkly. "What do you think?"

"I think there's a tender idealist buried somewhere deep inside you." Troy grinned crookedly. "But I won't tell anyone."

"And I was just about to compliment you for doing a good thing here in this town."

"The ball?"

"The Graff."

"Huh."

"Marietta didn't need the Graff, but you've done something this town can be proud of. And that's a good thing."

"Maybe you should have been my date Friday night," Troy said.

"You are pretty, but you're not quite my type."

Troy laughed. "I'm crushed."

TAYLOR COULDN'T WAIT for work to end Wednesday. She was looking forward to meeting up with McKenna and going dress shopping at Married in Marietta, because now Taylor needed a dress, too.

It'd been a long time since Taylor did something like this. Even longer since she'd needed to dress up for something. For the last couple of years she'd been focused on work, and getting Doug the help he needed. There hadn't been time for dates or dances, and in trying to be responsible and mature she'd also somehow lost being young and fun.

Maybe for one night she could just forget about being Doug's guardian and remaining on guard and keeping a vigilant watch. Maybe for one night she could cut loose and leave Hogue to worry about Doug and she could just relax…have fun. She wasn't trying to ignore her responsibilities. She just wanted a mini break. A chance to dress up and play. Surely it'd be okay for just one night.

Taylor must have looked at her watch a dozen times between three and five, and the minute hand never seemed to move. She felt as if she'd gotten a case of spring fever, but finally it was five, and Louise, aware that Taylor was going to the ball with Troy, shooed her out the door, promising Taylor she'd lock up since Margaret had gone home with a toothache earlier in the day.

Taylor headed home to change from her trousers and knit sweater set to jeans and a peach cotton sweater that was cut boxy and loose in a boyfriend style, before combing her hair and leaving it loose.

Hoping she was dressed appropriately for a girl's night out with McKenna, Taylor drove to Married in Marietta on Front Ave and snagged a parking spot just a block from the store.

Taylor had never been inside the little boutique before, but passing through the front door was like entering another world, an overtly feminine world with a pale plush carpet, soothing neutrals, glittering chandeliers and delicate French inspired furniture.

A sales associate came forward to greet Taylor and offer assistance. "I'm looking for a dress for Friday night," Taylor said.

The sales clerk gestured to the long wall filled with fluffy and shimmering white gowns at the back. "That is our bridal area," she said, before pointing to four rolling racks of gowns in pink, coral and red, "and over there are the formal gowns we've ordered in for the Valentine Ball. We have a little bit of everything here, and I do have more sizes in the back."

Taylor thanked her and headed for the rolling racks of rose and ruby gowns, some filmy and chiffon, others short and fitted, while others sparkled with sequins and embroidery. They seemed to have something for every taste, and hopefully every budget since Taylor didn't have much money.

"Hope you haven't been waiting long," McKenna said, a little breathless as she appeared at Taylor's side, her cheeks red from the cold. She quickly began peeling off her heavy outer layers. "TJ gave me fits tonight. He decided he didn't want me to go out and made quite a scene."

Taylor turned to McKenna, worried. "Will he be okay?"

"Yes. He just likes throwing his weight around." McKenna grimaced as she placed her coat and scarf and gloves on a fragile white chair. "He's only four but he's already all Sheenan. Not sure why I thought he'd end up with any of my DNA."

"Until last night, I didn't realize his dad was Trey."

"Troy told you?"

Taylor shook her head. "Louise."

"Not a planned pregnancy. But then, my life doesn't seem to follow any logical plans." McKenna shrugged and turned her focus to the racks of dresses. She rifled through the nearest rack before pausing at a strapless, fitted peach gown covered in sequins that gave way to a silk skirt at the thigh. "How pretty. So romantic."

"I've never worn gowns like these," Taylor said, "at least, not since the Hopeville High prom, and even then, I chose a simple off white dress that seemed classic and elegant. At least, I thought I looked pretty and elegant until I got to the gym and realized the dress looked like a sheet off my parents' bed."

McKenna laughed and pulled out a short, miniscule pink sequin cocktail dress. "I think I wore something like this to my prom."

THE TYCOON'S KISS

"Very sexy," Taylor said.

"Mmm. Short, tight, sexy with the highest heels I could find. I wanted to drive Trey crazy."

"Did he love it?"

"No." McKenna hung the shimmering pink number back on the rack. "He was livid." She looked at Taylor, and scrunched her nose. "He wasn't my date. We'd broken up the week before but I refused to sit home crying. So my brother, Quinn, the baseball star, found a date for me, and I went to my prom looking like a million bucks with one of his friends. It made Trey nuts."

"Did you and Trey get back together after the prom?"

"We did, towards the end of summer. But broke up again by Christmas. Didn't date again for a year since Trey was competing on the circuit." McKenna's smile faded. "We were impossible. Our relationship was impossible. We shouldn't have ever let it go on as long as we did."

McKenna turned back to the rack and quickly flipped through more gowns but Taylor had seen the tears in McKenna's eyes.

"But you're happy now, right?" Taylor asked, worriedly. "You're newly engaged and getting married later this year, so it's okay?"

McKenna held a sleek dark pink gown against her slender frame. The long dress was cut asymmetrical with one shoulder strap and a sequin starburst at the waist. McKenna might not be a dress girl, but she was certainly drawn to gorgeous sexy gowns. "What do you think?"

Taylor noticed McKenna hadn't answered her question. "Very pretty. And that dark coral pink looks great with your hair."

"They always say redheads shouldn't wear pink, but I don't believe in following rules."

"I think it's gorgeous."

"So explain to me why you're not going to the ball," McKenna asked, handing the dresses to the sales clerk who carried them to a dressing room.

"Well, actually…I am going…now."

"Good! Great. So you're dress shopping, too. Let's find some things for you to try on. Have you seen anything you like? What's your style?"

"Inexpensive?"

McKenna gave Taylor a pointed look. "No woman wants to look cheap."

"No, I know, but I don't have a big budget."

"I'm sure we can find something pretty that won't break your budget. So what do you like? Long? Short? Fitted? Full? And are you a pink girl, or red, or apricot or purple?"

"I like red better than pink," Taylor said. "And apricot better than purple. And I don't know about the rest. Just pretty. I don't want to look like I'm wearing a sheet from my mother's bed."

"Got it."

For the next half hour they tried on dress after dress, and

took turns posing and turning in front of the tall mirror.

In the end McKenna chose the stunning pink asymmetrical gown with the starburst at the waist as it hugged her curves and set off her dark auburn hair, green eyes, and flawless, luminous skin.

"What about you?" McKenna asked. "What are your favorites?"

"I like the red lace cocktail dress," Taylor said, "and the ivory dress with the bronze sequins at the bodice. That was really pretty, too."

"The red lace dress is what old ladies wear to hide their jiggly upper arms," McKenna said, "and the ivory dress is pretty, but it looks like a bargain priced dress. Something for teens to wear to their prom. You're twenty-six and in June you'll be Marietta's new head librarian. You need a dress with wow factor, something that screams stylish, sexy, and sophisticated."

Taylor shook her head. "Not sexy. Definitely not sexy. Stylish and sophisticated is good enough."

"Why not sexy?" McKenna demanded, flipping through more hanging gowns, this time on a search for Taylor.

"Um, I'm not... sexy, and even if I was, I couldn't go to the ball looking too sexy. My date wouldn't like it."

McKenna turned to face Taylor, hands on her hips. "What? Why not?"

Taylor shifted from one foot to the other. "My date isn't a... date. We're really just friends, and so we're just going as… friends."

"I don't get it. Who are you going with?"

Taylor had wondered when this question might arise. "Troy."

"Troy *Sheenan*?"

Was there any other Troy in Marietta?

Taylor nodded. "Yes." She avoided McKenna's gaze, not wanting to see laughter or mockery in her eyes, because of course Troy wasn't the right man for Taylor. Troy was… well… Marietta's Most Eligible Bachelor. And probably San Francisco's Most Eligible Bachelor, too. "Jane set us up—"

"I knew Jane had said you were going."

"I didn't think it was a good idea to go with Troy, but anyway…we are."

"You and Troy."

"Yes." Taylor's heart thudded, trying not to think about Troy or the kiss, because the kiss had been so good and hot and sweet and sexy all at the same time. "But we're not a couple," she added hurriedly.

"Maybe you should be a couple. He's lovely," McKenna said firmly. "And you are, too."

"But there's no… chemistry," Taylor said, remembering Troy's words. "And he has to have chemistry. You know."

"How do you know there was no chemistry?"

Taylor blushed. "He kissed me."

McKenna's eyes widened. "And…?"

"I thought it was really good."

"Not surprised. He was voted best kisser his senior year of high school. And of course, *I* never kissed him, but Sheenans are good lovers, so, you know."

Taylor glanced around to be sure the sales clerk wasn't listening. "Apparently I'm not a good kisser, though. Troy said… you know."

"Troy told you that you weren't a good kisser?"

"No. He just said… we could be friends."

"Of course you can be friends. You don't want a lover who doesn't care about you."

"He's not my lover. He's not even attracted to me."

"And he said this?"

"*No.* But it was *implied.*"

McKenna gave her a strange look. "Not sure your logic is all that sound, which is fine. No one ever said a woman has to be logical all the time. But the one thing that is clear, is that we need to find you the perfect gown for the ball. Yes?"

In the dressing room, armed with another stack of gowns, all handpicked by McKenna, Taylor tried on one after the other. They were all beautiful dresses, all far more sophisticated than Taylor would have selected for herself. A stunning ruby red ball gown with full skirts and a plunging décolleté; a long, form fitting red sequin gown with small padded shoulders that left her entire back bare; a sweet gown in blush with avant garde roses stitched at the bodice and fluttery folds of fabric falling to her feet.

So many beautiful gowns and yet none of them felt right.

She couldn't imagine going to the ball in any of them. And then, right when Taylor didn't think she could try on another dress, the sales clerk pushed a dress through the curtain and insisted Taylor try it on. "This was in the back," the girl said. "It's a small size, but you're tiny and young enough to pull the look off."

Taylor warily eyed the gown with the red circle spangles. It was not a quiet little dress, nor a sleek sophisticated gown. It was… eye catching. Maybe even show stopping. It was a dress better suited to a stage or runway…

"It's not me," Taylor said, poking her head out of the dressing room. "It's just too much."

"Put it on," McKenna said.

"Do," the sales girl agreed. "I think you'd look beautiful in it. You have the right coloring with your dark hair and eyes. How can it hurt to give it a try?"

A few minutes later Taylor stepped from the dressing room and turned to let the sales girl zip up the back of the dress.

She shot McKenna a quick glance as she took a place before the tall mirror. McKenna's eyes were wide, and she was smiling, broadly.

Taylor looked from McKenna to the mirror, and studied her reflection.

And then she did a slow twirl in front of the mirror, unable to believe she was looking at herself.

She looked… incredible.

THE TYCOON'S KISS

It was the dress, of course. And the gown's tulle wasn't exactly pink, more blush or nude, and covered with those glossy red spangles and moved and shimmered and reflected the light.

Taylor put a hand to the deep V-neck bodice, and then to the full skirt.

"It's... pretty," she said softly, a bit awed by her own reflection.

"Stunning," the sales clerk agreed.

"That's the dress," McKenna added.

"I think so," Taylor agreed, before reaching for the tag that hung beneath her arm. She blinked, shocked by the price, and read it a second time, making sure she hadn't read it wrong. $3,900.

Three *thousand* and nine hundred dollars.

Good God. Did people really pay this much for a single dress? "It's way too much. Way, way too much."

"But it's perfect," McKenna said. "You look like a princess."

"Anyone would in a dress that costs almost four thousand dollars," Taylor retorted, turning around to be unzipped.

"What?" McKenna cried.

"I know," Taylor answered.

"It is couture," the sales girl said. "One of a kind."

"Not for me. I'm not couture," Taylor said, shaking her head. "I'm an off the rack kind of a girl. Eighty to one hundred dollars max on a dress. That's my budget. And the ivory dress with the bronze sequin bodice fit me, and my budget. I'll go with that."

## Chapter Seven

WITH DRESSES ZIPPED into garment bags and then stowed in their cars, McKenna and Taylor walked down 1st Avenue to Grey's Saloon on Main for drinks and appetizers.

"When does Jane return?" McKenna asked, as they settled into a booth towards the back of the saloon.

"Tomorrow afternoon," Taylor answered, glancing towards the pool tables where Callan Carrigan was playing with a couple of cowboys. Taylor had been told that Callan could outride and out rope virtually any local cowboy, and from the looks of it, she could out play them at pool, too. Callan's sure shots were sending ball after ball into the pockets.

The guys let out a loud collective groan and McKenna turned to watch Callan take a bow. "Looks like Callan kicked butt again," McKenna said.

"She's nothing like Sage, is she?" Taylor said, secretly rather intimidated by Callan, even though they were practically the same age.

"Nope. But none of the Carrigan girls are alike. Just as the Sheenan brothers are all so different." McKenna turned back around, faced Taylor. "Speaking of the Sheenans, just how is it that Jane set you up with Troy?"

"I'm not sure. It was all Jane's doing, not my idea at all." Taylor glanced up, happy to see the waitress with their drinks. Taylor could use a drink right about now, and that was saying something since she was always careful about drinking. Never have more than two. Now all they needed was some food and things would be perfect.

"Help me understand why Troy needed an arranged date?" McKenna persisted.

"Jane said Troy's dad was dying and Troy and his girl-friend had just broken up so Jane was making sure Troy had a date for his own ball."

"Seems odd to me that Jane would set you up with him, when I think she had a thing for Troy."

"She did," Taylor agreed. "But apparently now they are just friends."

"Hmmm." McKenna touched her finger to the salt rimming her glass. "I'd love to know Troy's take on all that."

"He claims it was one-sided. He cares about Jane, but nothing more."

"I believe it." McKenna licked the salt from her fingertip. "Jane's not his type."

"Why not? She's really smart and successful and—"

THE TYCOON'S KISS

"A little too abrasive."

"Jane's not abrasive."

McKenna gave her a look. "You have to admit that Jane's a little pushy."

Taylor shrugged uneasily. "It's her job to get things done."

"Fair enough, but she's not his type. Now you...you could be Troy's type."

"No."

"Troy liked sweet girls, sweet, smart, successful girls. Nice girls who also happen to be very smart." She lifted her glass, sipped her margarita, green eyes gleaming. "Girls like you."

Taylor nearly choked on her wine. "He doesn't like me."

"He must like you if he's kissed you."

"He kissed me as a test. It was to see if we had chemistry."

"I see. And this is the test you claim you failed?"

"Yes."

McKenna laughed quietly and then sipped her margarita again. "He's playing you."

"He's not."

"Troy Sheenan would never kiss you if there wasn't a little spark. If he felt absolutely no attraction, he wouldn't even bother with a kiss." McKenna shook her glass, letting the ice cubes clink. "Where were you when you kissed?"

"Main Street Diner."

"What?"

"That's what I mean. It wasn't a romantic kiss. He leaned across the table and kissed me to see if there were any… sparks."

"He did this all at Main Street Diner?"

"Yes."

McKenna grinned. "Good Lord, girl. He's definitely interested. He would never kiss you, much less take you to a ball if he wasn't."

"Remember, Jane arranged the ball part."

"But I know Troy and he doesn't do pity dates." McKenna's arched brows rose higher. "Troy Sheenan doesn't have to."

"Maybe not a pity date, but it's not a *date* date. That's why he kissed me. To make sure we could be friends, and so that's what we are."

"But you liked kissing him."

Taylor blushed. "He knows what he's doing."

"You just need confidence."

"I am confident."

"Maybe as a librarian, but not as a woman." McKenna suddenly leaned forward, and reaching out, plucked the glasses from Taylor's nose. "Why do you wear these all the time now? You didn't used to."

"I need them," Taylor answered, sticking her hand out, palm up. "May I have them back?"

"When you first moved here, you hardly ever wore your

THE TYCOON'S KISS

glasses. Now I never see you in contacts."

"I like my glasses," Taylor said a little stiffly. "And I can't see you right now, so I'd like them back."

McKenna put them in her hand. "Here you go. And don't be mad. I wasn't trying to be hurtful. I'm just curious. And maybe concerned."

"Concerned, why?"

"I don't know. I just kept thinking that maybe something happened." She must have seen Taylor's expression because she quickly added, "I get the feeling that you're hiding, or just hiding behind the glasses. But maybe I'm wrong. Maybe I'm just... projecting."

A whistle from the pool tables drew Taylor's attention and she glanced over at Callan who had her hand out, collecting dollar bills. It seemed she'd just won another game.

"I'm not hiding anything," Taylor said after a moment. "Just trying to... look... older."

"Why?"

Taylor shrugged. "I was told back in early December that I didn't look mature enough. That I was too young. So I'm trying to dress more age appropriately."

"Age appropriate for what? Too young for what? Take over Margaret's job as head librarian?"

"No." Taylor hesitated, her heart pounding a little too fast, making her suddenly queasy. She really didn't like discussing Doug with others. Family dynamics were difficult enough without other people weighing in. "Take care of my brother."

"You have a younger brother?"

"He's not a child. He's twenty-two. He's... at Hogue Ranch."

McKenna's forehead creased. "That work ranch, halfway house place out in Paradise Valley?"

Taylor nodded again. "He's been there since early September, and he had a chance to be released before Christmas. He was supposed to come live with me, but the judge didn't think I was old enough, and mature enough, to manage my brother—who happens to have some problems—so instead of letting Doug spend the six month probation period with me, he said Doug had to stay at Hogue."

"What did your brother do?"

"He wasn't respectful to an officer."

"I don't understand. Did he hurt someone? Attack someone?"

"No. He was argumentative with a local sheriff who pulled him over for driving too fast. They booked him, and drug tested him and he tested positive for marijuana. He tried to explain that he was argumentative because the sheriff treated him like he was an idiot, and he's not, he was just scared and uncomfortable, and then they labeled him as some loser, and he's not a loser, either. Doug said in court that he sometimes smokes to manage his depression but the judge said this isn't Colorado or California. If he wants to be

THE TYCOON'S KISS

a drug addict, go there." Taylor swallowed hard, and again. "Hogue isn't a good place for him. It's hard core. Most men there have been in and out of jail a couple of times, but Doug's not a criminal. He has clinical depression."

"Is that what you told the judge?"

"I told the judge that Doug needed help. Counseling. Better depression medicine. Or a better dose of his medicine. But the judge dismissed everything I said, claiming that I was too young, and too immature, to know what was right for my brother."

McKenna regarded her for a long moment. "You're angry."

"I am." Taylor drew a slow breath and blinked, clearing her vision. "If I were a man, the judge wouldn't have talked to me like I was a little girl. If I'd been a local, I can guarantee that my brother wouldn't be at Hogue right now. My brother would be living with me. Kara even said as much after it was all over."

"Kara Jones? The district attorney?"

"She's my roommate. Well, house mate. I rent a room from her, and have been living there since I arrived in Marietta last November."

"And Kara couldn't help you?"

"No. Conflict of interest."

"You'd think the judge would see that as a plus on your side. You live with Marietta's DA!"

"Kara wanted me to ask one of the local ranching families like the MacCreadies or Carrigans or even the Sheenans to hire Doug. She thought Brock Sheenan would be the perfect person to approach. She said everyone knows Brock, and Brock's solid and no-nonsense, and went to school with the judge's daughter, but I was afraid to approach him. Brock didn't know me from Adam and it made me nervous to get strangers involved. It still does. Doug's had a hard life. My parents treated him different than me. They were not loving towards him—" Taylor broke off, bit down into her lower lip to hold the tears back. "He's spent his life struggling to come to terms with their rejection, and he's allowed to have feelings and be frustrated and figure out who he is, and what he wants, without all of Crawford County judging him."

McKenna waited a moment before speaking. "But you know Brock now," she said quietly. "You've met him, you've met Harley. He has a big spread, too, and is always looking for help, particularly in the spring. He's got a foreman who has been with him a long time, and his hands are all good people. He'll be hiring a few new guys soon. This would be the time to talk to him."

"But it's too late now. Doug has to remain at Hogue until the end of May."

"Or not." McKenna held her gaze. "I think you should hire a good attorney and let your friends here in Marietta help you."

Taylor said nothing and McKenna reached across the

THE TYCOON'S KISS

table and tapped her arm.

"Are you listening?" McKenna asked.

Taylor looked up at her. "I am, but McKenna, you grew up here, everybody cares about you here. I'm not Marietta's sweetheart. I'm a nobody here."

"*I* can help you."

"How?"

"I can go to Brock or Cormac or Troy—"

"*No*."

"Why not?"

"Because I'm not going to beg for favors from the Sheenans. That's wrong. They don't know me—"

"You're going to the ball with Troy!"

"I explained this already. I'm going with Troy because Jane forced us together."

"Phooey. Open your eyes. Use your brain." McKenna drummed her hand on the table. "Nobody forces Troy to do anything. Not even Trey could get Troy to do something Troy didn't want to do. And Trey was persuasive, and stubborn, but Troy is strong. Troy doesn't take crap from anyone, and he doesn't play games. If he likes you, he likes you, and if he doesn't, he avoids you. And if you're going to the ball with him, it's because he wanted to take you, and if he's kissed you, it's because he wanted to put his lips on your lips. Nobody made him."

Taylor hung her head, embarrassed. She knew McKenna was looking at her but Taylor didn't know what to say, or

121

how to articulate her feelings. It was hard enough worrying about her brother and struggling to come to terms with how he'd been rejected by her parents and society, without her having to deal with rejection, too.

It was a challenge coming to terms with Doug's depression, and supporting him through his disappointments without her feeling disappointed in herself.

Without her feeling disappointed in her dreams.

Better to not want too much or dream too big.

Better to keep one's expectations small, and manageable.

Better to do everything yourself because you couldn't always rely on others.

"Why are you so afraid to like Troy?" McKenna asked quietly.

Taylor pictured him—tall and so darkly handsome—in his long black wool coat and fitted cashmere sweater stepping from his big black Escalade. The man had a private jet. He lived in some outrageous mansion in the most affluent neighborhood in San Francisco. He lived in a world she didn't know and didn't understand and would never be part of. "He has so much."

"Yes?"

"I have nothing. I rent a room in a house on Bramble and am lucky to be able to pay my bills each month, while he has a private jet. A *jet*. It's embarrassing how different our circumstances are."

"You're not into material things. Even if you had the

THE TYCOON'S KISS

money, you wouldn't spend it on fancy toys, but it's also okay if he has toys. You don't have to focus on the stuff, focus on him. Are you attracted to him?"

Taylor shifted uncomfortably. "I've never met anyone like him," she admitted.

"Is that good or bad?"

She hesitated only a second. "It's good."

"So stop letting grumpy old Judge McCorkle turn you into a timid little field mouse. Have confidence. Enjoy life. Enjoy your life. You're beautiful—"

"I think that's going too far."

"It's not. You're really pretty, Taylor. You could even be very sexy if you just lost the sweater sets, grandma pearls, and men's glasses."

"I don't want to be sexy, but even if I did dress like a hipster, Troy would still be this city slicker—"

"You don't know Troy. He's not a city slicker." McKenna sounded almost frosty. "Yes, he lives in San Francisco but that's because he's brilliant and innovative and it's where technology and opportunity are, but that doesn't mean he's not real, and solid. Because he is. He's smart…loving…loyal. He's a wonderful man and he deserves to be treated like a man, and not like a shallow, insincere playboy."

Taylor flushed, hearing the criticism in McKenna's voice. "I've never said Troy is an insincere playboy."

"No?"

"I just don't think we're suited."

"Maybe because you haven't even given him a chance."

Taylor took a long drink from her wine glass, nearly draining it. The wine warmed her, and gave her courage. She set her glass down with a little thunk and looked at McKenna. "If you're such a Troy Sheenan fan, why didn't you fall for Troy, instead of Trey? Why wasn't Troy the right Sheenan?"

But the moment the words left her mouth, Taylor knew they were the wrong words. She'd said the wrong thing. Taylor didn't even need to see McKenna's face to know she'd hurt McKenna, she could just feel it in the air and the sudden heaviness at the table.

Worse, McKenna said nothing and Taylor's stomach was now filled with knots. "I'm sorry," Taylor whispered, ashamed of herself for saying something so flippant and thoughtless when McKenna had been nothing but kind to Taylor since she'd moved here at the end of the summer. "That was terrible. Forgive me."

"It's okay."

"No, it's not."

"It is, and actually, it's a very good question," McKenna said, smiling faintly. But the smile didn't reach her eyes. "I'm sure everyone wonders the same thing. Why didn't I fall in love with Troy? My life would have been so different. So much… *easier*." McKenna pushed her glass away from her and glanced at her watch. "Oh dear, it's late. I need to go. My sitter has a big test tomorrow. I promised I wouldn't keep her out too late."

"I should go, too," Taylor said, rising, still kicking herself

THE TYCOON'S KISS

for ruining the mood, and maybe the evening, too. "I really am sorry, McKenna. I shouldn't have been so sensitive, and I shouldn't have said what I did—"

"Stop. It's okay," McKenna said firmly, cutting the apology off. "I'm fine. No harm done. Honestly. And yes, you should speak up. Speak your mind. You can't go through life minimizing yourself, marginalizing yourself, hoping it will please others." She wagged her finger at Taylor, a hint of her good humor returning. "I used to be a big sister, and so I'll tell you what I would have told my sister, Fiona Grace. Don't live to please others. Don't think everyone else knows what's right or true. Listen to yourself, and be true to yourself. That way, no matter what else happens in life, you will always have your self-respect."

McKenna finished buttoning her coat and slipped her gloves on. "And I don't know why I didn't fall for Troy," she added thoughtfully as they started for the door. "Troy is everything Trey isn't. He's good, he's kind, he's responsible. *Successful.* He doesn't drink too much and he doesn't get into bar fights—" She broke off, pursed her lips, and shook her head. "No. He's nothing like Trey, which is why he doesn't make my heart race or my pulse quicken or make me feel special, and beautiful, and new. And Trey made me feel that. From day one. From day one Trey made me feel like I was the most amazing girl in the world." Her shoulders lifted and fell. "How can you not love a man that makes you feel like a goddess… absolutely divine?"

## Chapter Eight

TROY WAS GLAD that the uncomfortable ninety-minute dinner with Judge McCorkle at the Graff was over and he was now free to sit at the bar at Grey's and just relax.

Ninety minutes wasn't long when you were dining with friends or a beautiful woman, but ninety minutes was endless when you were being solicited for a loan.

Judge Joe McCorkle found himself on the wrong side of a business deal and was in financial trouble. Of course he didn't want anyone in the community to know he'd made some mistakes with his investments, and that he'd already taken out a second mortgage on his house to sort things out only to have just dug himself deeper into debt. He'd already approached both local banks and Big Sky Credit Union, and all three had turned him down. Judge McCorkle was a risk. He was also nearing retirement. How could he ever pay the loan back?

For that matter, how could he save his house? His wife had no idea that they could soon lose their home, and

THE TYCOON'S KISS

everything they'd worked for.

Troy had listened to all this over a dinner of steak and whiskey. He paid for the dinner. The judge had no money.

The judge knew Troy had money.

What was a two hundred and fifty thousand dollar loan between friends? Hadn't Troy gone to school with his daughter Susie? (And no, Troy hadn't. Brock had.)

Troy hadn't told the judge yes. But he hadn't told him no. He had to think about it. Had to figure out where the money would come from, and be realistic about McCorkle's ability to pay him back.

The judge might not ever be able to pay him back.

This wasn't the first time Troy was approached by a Marietta individual needing assistance. It wouldn't be the last.

As Troy entered Grey's, he spotted a half dozen different people he knew. Callan Carrigan was in the far back, shooting pool, with a couple of Brock's young hired hands. Dawson O'Dell and a young off duty sheriff were eating burgers at a table on one side, while McKenna and Taylor were having drinks on the other side.

Interesting, seeing McKenna and Taylor together. He knew from last night that they were going dress shopping together but he hadn't expected to see them.

They were talking, quite seriously, from the looks of things. He hoped they'd had a good evening. McKenna would be a good friend for Taylor. McKenna didn't bullshit and she wasn't superficial, and she was the first to stand up for the underdog.

Even more interesting was seeing McKenna head his way now.

"Hey," McKenna said, coming to the bar counter to greet him.

"Hey, yourself," he said, sliding off the stool. "Hello, Taylor," he added, nodding at the librarian who was hanging back, as if to give them space. Troy turned his attention to McKenna. "You okay?"

She tucked a long dark red strand of hair behind her ear. "Sorry about last night."

"It's fine."

"I wanted to talk to you, but it's… weird."

"I get it."

She shook her head, jaw set, frustration evident. "It's always such a shock… seeing you… even now. I know you can't help looking like him, the rat bastard."

Troy reached out and folded McKenna into a quick hug. "The curse of being an identical twin," he said, dropping a kiss on the top of her head.

"I should hate you," she said, her voice muffled against his chest.

"You should."

She looked up at him, smiling faintly, crookedly. "I don't."

"That's good." He released her, and watched as she

THE TYCOON'S KISS

stepped back, moving closer to Taylor. McKenna had been a very pretty girl and she'd grown into an absolutely stunning woman with long auburn hair, light green eyes, high cheekbones and a perfect chin, beneath perfect lips. But beneath her beauty was sadness. Her fire and courage didn't completely mask her pain. McKenna had lived through a terrible tragedy and then she'd fallen in love with a man who couldn't get his shit together long enough to protect her properly so that her wounds could heal. Instead Trey just kept hurting her, making the scars and pain worse.

"How's TJ?" Troy asked. "Is he doing okay?"

"He's smart as a whip. And a chip off the old block."

"Lucky you."

"Haha."

Troy glanced at Taylor, not wanting to leave her out of the conversation and yet not sure how to include her, before focusing back on McKenna. "I'd love to come see him while I'm in town. If you're alright with that."

McKenna smiled. "That'd be great. He'd love seeing you." She hesitated. "But it is confusing for him. You look, you know, like his—" she broke off, smiled, even as tears glittered in her eyes. "So how is everyone? How's your dad?"

"Dad's not doing well. He's fading fast. I think it'd be a miracle if he makes it another two weeks."

"I'm sorry." She hesitated. "Do you think he'd want... to see... TJ?"

"I'm sure he would. Maybe we can bring TJ by this

weekend while I'm still home?"

She nodded and drew a deep breath. "I don't know if you've heard. I'm engaged, to Larry… Lawrence… Joplin."

"Dillon told me."

McKenna glanced at Taylor, who was still hanging back, and then at Troy. "I have to do what's right for me and TJ."

"I understand."

"TJ needs stability and security. *I* need stability and security."

"We all understand. We do. And we support you. We love you."

McKenna's eyes narrowed and she looked away, focusing very hard on a distant point across the bar. "I haven't told Trey. I'm not going to."

"Okay."

McKenna glanced at Taylor again, and struggled to smile. "I understand you're taking Taylor to the ball."

Troy saw Taylor's eyes widen behind her big glasses. She looked positively mortified. "Yes," he said, checking his smile. "Taylor has most graciously agreed to accompany me to the ball."

"That was very nice of her," McKenna said, lips curving. "And that's because she's a *nice* girl, Troy, not like your big city floozies. So please, Troy, be on your best behavior Friday night." She winked and walked out.

MCKENNA EXITED GREY'S front door so fast, Taylor didn't

have a chance to follow. But then, after McKenna's teasing final remarks, Taylor had no desire to follow.

"That was so unbelievably awkward," she murmured, her face hot, certain her cheeks were red.

Troy grinned down at her. "The family history, or the comment about my floozies?"

Heat washed through her all over again. "I don't care about the family history, or if you date floozies. In fact, good for you if you do."

She started for the door but Troy, reached out, grabbed the hood on her winter coat and kept her from escaping.

"Where are you going so fast?" he asked.

"Home." She tugged on her coat, trying to free herself. "And I've just hurt McKenna's feelings so let go, before I hurt yours."

He let her go. "Why did you hurt her feelings?"

Taylor exhaled and shook her head, still upset with herself. "She was being so nice and I'm not that nice. I'm not. And so I said something I shouldn't have, and I think it made her sad."

"What did you say?"

"You don't want to know." She jammed her hands into her coat pockets and hunched her shoulders. "I still feel terrible for saying it."

"Now you have to tell me. What did you say to her?"

Taylor's shoulders rose higher. "She kept talking about you... paying you all these compliments and it was frustrating and so I said… that if she liked you so much, why Trey? Why not you?"

Troy sighed. "Probably wasn't the best thing to say, no, but if it's any comfort, I don't think you hurt her feelings as much as touched on a tender spot. People have been saying that to her for years about Trey and me. But she and I are just friends, and what she and Trey had was… special. It's hard to explain but they just… worked. She adored him, and he her."

"So what happened?"

"Trey loves adrenaline. He takes risks and lives recklessly. It was hard on McKenna, never knowing if he was in trouble, or safe. She worried about him on the rodeo circuit, worried about him drinking, worried about him fighting. It just wore her down, and it made Trey defensive." He sat back down on his bar stool and extended his long legs out, arms crossing over his big chest. "So how did the dress shopping go? Did she find something?"

"We both did."

"You both did," he repeated, confused.

She nodded, looking self-conscious. "I hadn't bought a gown yet."

Suddenly he understood. The ball. They'd gone dress shopping for the Valentine Ball. McKenna hadn't been shopping for her wedding gown. Relief swept through him. "Tell me about your dress."

"No."

THE TYCOON'S KISS

"Why not?"

"You'll see it Friday night."

"But you love it?"

Taylor flushed. "I wouldn't say I loved it, but's nice."

"A nice dress for a nice girl. Sounds incredibly sexy."

She rolled her eyes. "As we've just established, I'm not that nice. And the dress *is* nice. It's appropriate for the ball."

"So it's a ball gown?"

"*No.* At least, it's not how I'd describe a ball gown, but I'm not going to spend a fortune on a dress I can only wear once, so I bought a dress that's pretty. It's long. Formal. And I could still wear it to other things in the future."

"Like what?"

"Are you really this interested in a dress, or are you just giving me a hard time?"

The deep husky laugh seemed to rumble from his chest. "Maybe I'm just interested in you."

"That's ridiculous."

"You are such a prickly little pear, Miss Harris."

Taylor ignored that. Wasn't even going to dignify his comment with a response. "Maybe I couldn't wear my dress to a wedding, since it's off-white and that's kind of a no-no, but I could wear it to another black-tie event."

"Because you go to so many of those," he teased, his gaze resting on her lips, making her lips feel tingly and hot.

She looked away, had to look away, flooded with emotions and sensation she didn't want. She didn't trust any of this. Troy was charming and obviously good at banter, but she did feel out of her league. Gorgeous men didn't flirt with her. Gorgeous men never even looked at her. "I might in the future," she said crisply, glancing back at him and then swallowing hard when she discovered he was smiling at her. Not just a crooked little smile but a smile with his lips and eyes, one of those smiles that made his blue gaze warm. He had beautiful eyes, too, and right now they glowed with a teasing light, knowing light, as if he knew her.

But he didn't. He didn't know the first thing about her.

Correction. He did know a few things. He did know she didn't enjoy balls and black-tie events because she'd told him that. But other than that limited bit of knowledge, he knew very little else about her, and so he shouldn't smile at her with warm blue eyes and he shouldn't let his lips curve as if they were having a delightful, playful conversation.

Taylor swallowed hard, and pressed her lips together, trying not to think about how it'd felt when he kissed her at the diner—*so good*—and how he'd smelled—*delicious*—and how hard it had been to fall asleep last night when she kept thinking about going to the ball with him and dancing with him and having dinner at the Sheenan table with him and his brothers...

Her heart had raced. Just as it was racing now.

Her imagination had gone nearly wild, creating scenarios that could never happen. That would never happen. Swashbuckling heroes didn't fall in love with quiet librarians.

THE TYCOON'S KISS

Not unless they'd had a learning disability and needed help with reading. Or filing.

She frowned, watching as he leaned back and dragged a hand through his dark hair, ruffling it. His blue denim shirt, rolled back on his wrist, slid towards his elbow, revealing dense, corded muscle in his forearm and lightly tanned skin.

Shameless. He was.

His gaze met hers, held. His lips curved into a wider, crooked smile. His expression seemed to say that he was enjoying her right now, and maybe even enjoying her a great deal.

Which couldn't be.

It didn't make sense. It didn't work. It wasn't real or plausible.

And did he do this to all women, smile at them and flirt and seduce them with his eyes? Seduce them with the curve of his firm lips?

Taylor wouldn't be surprised if he did. Apparently back in high school, he was quite the expert kisser. He'd probably graduated in college to expert lover.

Annoying. So terribly annoying.

"Why are you frowning at me, Miss Harris?" he drawled, a lock of dark ruffled hair falling forward, giving him a rakish appearance.

"You're such a flirt," she said primly, glancing away, unable to hold his gaze, unnerved by the tension between them.

She felt hot and cold, jittery and nervous, and a little bit dizzy, too. He was projecting some kind of energy, a magnetic energy, and it had heat and intensity and confused the heck out of her.

He laughed softly. "I'm not."

"You are. And apparently you've always been one. Voted Best Kisser your senior year."

"As well as Most Likely to Succeed," he added.

"A truly talented man."

He held up his hands. "To be fair, the vote could have been rigged. My girlfriend was the yearbook editor, and there was some speculation after the results were announced that she stuffed the ballot box."

"You're incorrigible."

"I can't think of anything sexier than a beautiful woman with a great vocabulary."

She laughed because she had to. There was nothing else she could do. "You're also impossible."

"I've heard that. And for your information, I have always liked book girls. Smart girls. Newspaper editor. Yearbook editor. Girl with the highest GPA. Girl with the perfect SAT score. Girl with the biggest brain."

She laughed and pushed her glasses up on the bridge of her nose. "Book girls, huh?"

"Book girls with glasses."

"Stop." But she was smiling and feeling easier, better, than she had all day and she was looking forward to the ball Friday, more now than she ever had. "And I should go. We have an early morning staff meeting tomorrow—it's every Thursday—but tomorrow I'm supposed to present a report on the books I'm recommending we purchase this summer."

"That's exciting."

"Yes, except that Margaret will say we have no money so we can't buy any of them."

"Not as exciting."

"No, but I can try."

"Where are you parked? Can I walk you to your car?"

"No. I'm just down over a block. I'm good."

"I think I should walk you there."

"I don't think it's necessary. Marietta has a population of what? Ten thousand?"

"Give or take a few."

"I'm safe."

"You're sure?"

"I'm positive."

"Text me when you reach your car."

"I don't have your number."

"Then we need to correct that immediately," he said, fishing into his pocket for his phone. He scrolled through contacts, typed a message and hit send. "Now you do."

Taylor's phone buzzed in her satchel. She opened her satchel and took out her phone, reading the new text. *Save this number*, it read.

Smiling, she added the number to her contacts. "Saved."

"Don't you feel better now?"

"I'm not sure," she said, and it was a lie, because she felt positively fizzy and warm and wonderful on the inside. "And how did you get my number in the first place?"

"Jane."

"Ah." She blushed. She couldn't help it. "Good night, Troy."

"Good night, beautiful."

TROY WATCHED TAYLOR leave, her long dark hair hanging halfway down her back, her brown coat hitting at her hip, giving him an excellent view of her legs. She had great legs. He liked her very much in jeans. He thought he'd probably like her very much out of jeans as well...

Grey set Troy's beer in front of him. "Anything else?" Grey asked.

Troy shook his head. "Nope."

"Alright." Grey moved.

Troy took a sip of his beer. The glass was thick and chilled. The beer was perfectly cold, a hint of ice, but not too frosty. This was exactly what he needed after a depressing dinner with McCorkle and a flirtatious conversation with his favorite librarian.

He'd only just taken a second sip when suddenly Callan Carrigan was at his side, ordering a beer and taking a seat on the bar stool next to his.

"Look whose back in town," Callan said, turning on the bar stool to face him even as she waved off the chilled glass to

THE TYCOON'S KISS

drink straight from the bottle. "Troy Sheenan, the venture capitalist himself."

Troy gave Callan a long look as she downed nearly one third of the bottle.

He liked Callan. He'd seen a fair amount of her growing up as she and Dillon used to chum around, despite their parents' disapproval. But the Carrigan girls weren't topics of conversation at their house. In fact, the Carrigans were never to be mentioned in their house. The feud between the families had been strong. If Dillon or one of the other boys mentioned Callan or another of the girls, Mom would leave the table in tears, and Dad would start in on his lectures. Or worse.

Troy watched Callan take another long swig from the bottle. Her bottle was nearly empty.

Something was definitely bugging Callan tonight.

"What's up, kid?" Troy asked, taking a sip from his glass, deliberately dropping the nickname he and Trey had given her way back when, a nickname that always fired her up.

Her eyebrows lifted. "Kid, huh? You do know I'm practically running the Circle C these days?"

"Trailing in your dad's shadow, more like." Troy was just teasing but Callan wasn't in the mood.

"You want to piss me off, don't you?"

He gave her another long look over the rim of his glass. She was slender with dark hair that she usually wore in a ponytail—except when she was at the bar on a Friday night looking for trouble. Her slight boyish build made her look far younger than her twenty-five years. But her tight jeans and tank top showed off her curves all the same. "So what's going on? Why are you here? I would have thought you'd be home doing your nails and getting all dolled up for the big Valentine Ball."

"I'm not going to the ball, and even if I was, I wouldn't be getting my nails or hair done. And it wouldn't take me two days to get ready. Wouldn't even take me two hours. I'd just shower, put on my dress and boots and go."

He shook his head, checked his smile. She was still a sassy, smart-mouth thing, but he liked her sense of humor. He'd always found her refreshing. "So why aren't you going?" He nodded at the young cowboys standing around the pool table looking forlorn now that Callan had left. "Didn't any one of them ask you?"

"I have more fun here. Besides, the ball's expensive. Two hundred bucks a couple."

"And you're telling me no cowboy was willing to scrounge up two hundred bucks to take you?"

Her cheeks flushed pink. She glanced away, lips compressing. "I was asked. But I said no."

"Wrong guy?"

She shot him a sharp look. "Is there ever a right guy?"

"You don't like men now?"

She gave him another severe look. "Just because I can ride and rope better than any cowboy my age doesn't mean

I'm gay."

"Never said you were."

"Good, because I'm not. I just don't feel like dating and doing the whole romance thing right now." She pushed her empty beer bottle across the counter, away from her, and signaled to Grey that she wanted another. "Trying to come to terms with something and it's not easy. I'm mad. And confused. But mostly mad."

"Want to tell me about it?"

She laughed once. "You might regret saying that."

He already was. But, he couldn't back out now. "Tell me. If it'd make you feel better."

"I don't know *what* could make me feel better. Except maybe another beer."

Grey arrived, with the needed beer. He popped off the cap and slid the bottle across the counter to her.

Callan snapped it up and took a sip.

Troy frowned. This wasn't normal Callan behavior and he didn't know what to make of it. "What's going on?"

She didn't answer immediately, but then she looked up at him, brows furrowed, expression grim. "I learned some dark Carrigan family secrets."

"How dark?"

"Pretty damn dark."

"Why don't you just tell me? Then I can get back to worrying about my own problems."

"You think this has nothing to do with you?"

Her words were full of challenge—so like Callan. "Maybe you should get to the point."

"Maybe I will. The thing is—our mom had an affair."

He stared at her. Was this the beer talking? He remembered Bev Carrigan as a very proper sort of woman. Beautiful, with nice manners and a gentle way about her. "You're talking nonsense, Callan. Maybe you should find a nice, gentlemanly cowboy to give you a ride home."

"I don't need a ride home. I plan on crashing on Sage's couch when I'm done here." Callan shredded the label off the bottle. "But first, hear me out. I want you to listen to my story."

"Your mom's been gone a long time. Why did this come up now?"

Callan's smooth jaw tightened, her expression fierce. "The timing sucks. I couldn't agree more. But with all that's been going on with Mattie and her husband—they split up this fall—Sage decided to come clean. Apparently she's been keeping this secret since she was only twelve years old."

Troy's head throbbed. He had enough drama with Trey in jail, and McKenna engaged, and Cormac trying to raise April and Daryl's baby as if he was daddy material when Cormac was the least likely of all the Sheenans to settle down.

And now Callan was throwing all her family stuff at him, too.

"Hang on," he said, rubbing at his temple. "Wes and

THE TYCOON'S KISS

Mattie are separated?"

"On their way to divorced."

"Too bad." He'd seen Wes at a few rodeos. The man knew how to ride a bull. But marriage—that could be harder. "So what does that have to do with Sage keeping a secret?"

"She thought Mattie might be more inclined to work out her troubles with Wes if she knew that our mother had an affair. And that it hadn't ended in divorce for our parents."

Twisted logic, in Troy's mind. But he could sort of see the connection. "How did Sage know her mom cheated on your dad?"

"She walked in on them."

Wow. That was pretty heavy. And life changing for a kid.

Kind of like him walking in and discovering his mom was dead.

"Sorry," he said gruffly. "That's shitty. For Sage, and for all of you."

Callan took another long drink. "Thing is, Troy, our mother was with your father."

Troy went cold all over.

For a moment he couldn't think, or speak. For a moment there was just silence, and then a buzzing in his head. The sound a radio station makes when you haven't dialed in properly to the right channel.

The buzzing continued unabated.

And he thought of his mom. Not his dad.

*Was this why?*

Was this the reason for her terrible sadness? For her endless loneliness?

Troy stared blindly down into the pale gold of his beer. He couldn't believe it.

And yet...

He could.

Bev Carrigan and his dad?

"You're sure?" he asked roughly.

"Yep." Her voice was quiet, her expression strained.

*Shit.*

He wished he'd never stopped in at Grey's. Wished he'd gone straight from dinner to his room. Wished he could have avoided this conversation tonight. Wished he could have avoided this conversation for the rest of his life. "Does everyone know?"

"No one knows. Just you, me, and my sisters."

He drank, and then set the glass down and pushed the half empty glass away. "Lucky you, me, and your sisters," he muttered, reaching for his wallet to drop a five and a couple ones on the counter.

He rapped his knuckles on the counter to let Grey know he was leaving and then glanced down at Callan who suddenly looked very small and young on the bar stool. "My dad's dying," he said bluntly.

She nodded once, her dark braid slipping across her

THE TYCOON'S KISS

shoulder. "Dillon told me."

"But you didn't tell Dillon about the affair?"

She shook her head. "He's the one who moved home to take care of your dad. Doesn't seem fair to lay this on him, too." She managed a tight, tough-girl smile. "But you're Troy, the V.C. I figured your big shoulders could handle the truth."

His big shoulders, he silently repeated, leaving the saloon a few minutes later. Sometimes they didn't feel very big at all.

He was opening the door to his SUV when his phone buzzed. Troy checked his phone. A text had just come in from Taylor.

*Forgot to text from my car, but I am home.*

He looked at the text a moment and smiled. *Are you wearing that adorable robe with the big pink pigs?* He texted in reply.

*You're just jealous that you don't have one.*

Troy grinned. *Good night, book girl.*

*Good night, city slicker.*

# Chapter Nine

IT TOOK TAYLOR a long time to fall asleep that night.

She wished she could blame caffeine or work worries on her inability to doze off, but it wasn't anything like that. She wasn't even worrying about Doug.

She couldn't sleep because she had Troy on her brain and the rational, practical part of her brain was lecturing her that it was most impractical to be lying awake at twelve fifteen, thinking about him. But then there was this other part of her brain, a very small but rebellious little part, encouraging her to remember their conversation at Grey's and then the fun, albeit brief, text exchange once she was home.

The little rebellious voice inside of her was reminding her that life wasn't always fun so she should enjoy the moments that were positive.

Right now, curled up in bed with a howling wind outside, she was wanting to throw her weight behind the rebel voice, particularly as it was often smashed under the guise of

THE TYCOON'S KISS

being responsible and doing the right thing.

But honestly, was it such a wrong thing to think about Troy Sheenan?

It's not as if she was really falling for him. It's not as if she was imagining happy-ever-afters. She was still grounded, practical, sensible Taylor. Still committed to small towns, crumbling libraries, great books, and taking care of one's family.

And it's not as if, by thinking of him, she was going to create any drama, or influence fate.

No one knew she was thinking of him.

She certainly wouldn't tell McKenna or Jane, or anyone else. Nor would she ever let Troy find out. (God help her.) But it was kind of fun to play tonight back in her head, skipping the uncomfortable parts like the whole McKenna-Troy-Trey conversation and jumping to the talking to Troy at the bar.

She could still see him leaning against the bar, smiling at her with those very dark, blue eyes. He had great eyes. A great face.

*Great* body.

Thinking about him made her feel warm on the inside. And just a tiny bit bubbly.

But no one had to know. And in the morning, when the morning arrived, she wouldn't allow herself to dwell on the warm bubbly part anymore.

In the morning she'd go back to being practical and disciplined. She'd become sensible Taylor, Marietta's librarian.

But that was the morning.

Tonight she was still free to wish…and dream.

THURSDAY AFTERNOON LOUISE came bounding up the stairs to the second floor landing where Taylor was adding some of the photos and memorabilia of Marietta in 1914 to the second floor display cabinet. Taylor had found them in a box in the library's storage vault and thought it was the perfect time to change displays with the Valentine Ball tomorrow launching the 100 year anniversary of the Great Wedding Giveaway.

"Does Margaret know you're doing this?" Louise asked, stooping to get a look at the faces in one of the photographs.

"Nope."

"She might not like it. She was very partial to the agriculture display. Her dad was a farmer."

"Yes, I know. But the display was almost twenty years old. I think a change is in order." Taylor sat back and dusted her hands on a soft cloth she'd picked up at the Mercantile on Main Street. "And what is she going to do? Fire me? She can't. She didn't hire me."

"You're feisty today."

"I'm just tired of tiptoeing around, afraid of incurring Margaret's displeasure. This library is in the dark ages. It's time it embraced change and technology. Kids read on iPhones and tablets and we should at the very least have new

THE TYCOON'S KISS

adult and young adult books available for them as downloads." And yes, Taylor silently added, she was still smarting after this morning's meeting where Margaret rejected every single book Taylor had suggested as an interesting read for the local teenagers. Margaret still thought Nancy Drew was the leading series for girls. She couldn't accept that young adults today might enjoy vampires, werewolves, witches or apocalyptic literature stories featuring strong heroines.

"Well, I support you," Louise said. "And you'll have a say in the librarian that's hired to replace me, so be patient and know that change is coming."

"I'm trying," Taylor answered, positioning a new black and white photo of Marietta High with its graduating class of 1914 against a trophy dated 1914 before straightening. "Where is Margaret by the way? Still at the dentist?"

"Yes."

"Good. And I'm finished here, so maybe she won't even notice. She rarely comes upstairs anymore."

"I'm glad you're finished here because you need to come down. Something's arrived for you. It's in the staff room."

"Books?"

"No."

"Magazines?"

"No."

"Information on the ALA conference this summer?"

"*No.*"

"What then?"

149

"Just come see," Louise said firmly, but still beaming and clearly quite excited about something.

Taylor dusted her hands off, closed and locked the glass cabinet door before following Louise downstairs, behind the circulation desk, through the small office to the tiny staff room behind.

Inside the staff room, hanging on the antique coat rack, was an enormous silver garment bag with ornate black calligraphy, *Married in Marietta.*

"Lisa Renee dropped it off herself," Louise said. "Just moments ago."

Taylor arched a brow. "It must be a mistake. I'm not getting married, nor do I know anyone getting married."

Louise rolled her eyes. "You know everyone's gone there for their formal gowns for the ball. As a matter of fact, you were there with McKenna last night. Miss Renee was not. Apparently one of her sales associates was."

"Yes, and the sales associate rang up my dress and the dress I bought is hanging in my closet at home right now."

"Maybe there was a mistake—"

"There was no mistake. I bought my dress. It's in my closet. This isn't for me."

"But it is. She brought this for you, and there's a card with your name on it," Louise said. "So open it. Read it. The suspense is killing me."

But Taylor didn't want to open the card. She suddenly knew who'd sent the dress and it wasn't McKenna, or Lisa

Renee, the elegant stylish manager who did all the ordering for the bridal boutique.

It was Troy. It had to be Troy. McKenna must have said something to him.

Taylor's jaw tightened as she reached for the little envelope tied to the hanger with a silver ribbon. She slid open the envelope's flap and pulled out the creamy white card.

*Book girls do it better in red spangles.*
*Troy*

Taylor's heart jumped. Her pulse raced. She knew even without unzipping the garment bag which dress she'd find.

The couture gown.

Taylor peeked into the bag. Glossy red spangles caught the light, glowing and shimmering within.

Her heart fell. She exhaled in a soft, disappointed whoosh.

"Look at that," Louise murmured.

"Mmm," Taylor agreed, blinking back tears. It was such a gorgeous gesture on Troy's part, so exciting, and she loved the thought... she did, but she couldn't keep it. Couldn't wear it. Couldn't ever accept such an expensive gift. "But I have to send it back."

But before Taylor could phone Married in Marietta, Margaret marched into the staff room.

"Troy Sheenan is here, Taylor. He apparently is interested in joining one of the book clubs. He asked specifically about the Tuesday Night Book Group. Personally I don't think it's the right place for him, but I'll leave that to you."

Taylor found Troy perusing the New and Notable bulletin board display across from the circulation desk, next to the library's theme table, this month's theme being Valentine's Day, with classic romance novels artfully arranged. *Jane Eyre. Wuthering Heights. Pride and Prejudice. Sense and Sensibility.*

Taylor had fully expected Margaret to reject the theme and choice of books. But she'd left it there, and said nothing.

A victory, in Taylor's mind.

"Thank you for the dress," Taylor said, joining Troy in front of the bulletin board display. "But I can't keep it. I can't even imagine ever accepting something so extravagant—"

"I didn't pay for it," he said, turning to face her. His chiseled jaw was shadowed with a day old beard.

Taylor was surprised how good he looked with a little scruff. She tucked her hands behind her back, fingers threading together. "I'm sure it's not on loan."

"No, it's a gift, from Lily Jewel, the designer. She wants you to wear it and we're to be photographed and Jane is to send the photos to all her big-wig publicist friends who will tweet and share and post the photos on every fashion blog imaginable, ensuring that Lily Jewel's dress is seen by all."

Taylor blanched. "That's a lot of pressure. Maybe it would have been better if you'd bought the dress after all."

"You don't have to wear Lily's gown. You have a very

THE TYCOON'S KISS

nice new dress from *Married in Marietta* at home."

She smiled at him. "Are you making fun of my nice new dress, that happens to be practical, *and* affordable?"

"Just a little bit."

"I see." But she couldn't stop smiling at him. He made her feel good on the inside. Bubbly. Happy. It didn't make sense. Opposites shouldn't attract. Big city tycoons shouldn't like small town librarians. Impulsively, she reached up to touch his scruffy jaw. His skin was warm, his jaw was hard, the black bristles sharp against her fingertips. "I kind of like this," she said.

He lifted a brow. "That's good, because I don't always like to shave."

"You... lazy?"

"Can't be clean shaven all the time. Where's the fun in that?"

"You do look rather... wicked."

"And that's appealing?"

She blushed, and then pinched herself for blushing. "Maybe."

"Why is it that nice girls like wicked boys?"

"McKenna says you're the good twin."

"McKenna has never kissed me. How would she know?"

She blushed again. Her heart was beating so fast that her head felt light. This wasn't supposed to be happening. She had been determined to be practical and realistic today. "You say the most outrageous things."

"I like to make you smile." He dipped his head, kissed her lips, a swift brief kiss that caught her off guard. "We're going to have fun tomorrow night," he murmured, before stepping back, putting distance between them just as Margaret rounded the corner.

He shot Margaret a quick glance, then looked back at Taylor, his blue gaze gleaming. "Thank you so much, Miss Harris, for the information about the book groups. I look forward to attending my first meeting. I've never been part of a book club before."

JANE ARRIVED AT the library just before closing and then stayed to visit with Taylor after Margaret and Louise had left.

The front door was locked and Jane leaned on the circulation desk, watching Taylor swiftly swap out issues of magazines from the plastic protective covers.

"These are all Cormac Sheenan publications," Jane said, tapping the glossy new issues stacked in front of Taylor. "*Montana Living, Wyoming Living, Colorado Living,* and *Big Sky Design.*"

"We carry a couple more of his," Taylor said, clicking the plastic binder open, and taking out the January/February issue of *Big Sky Design* for the new March/April issue. "I think they are sport oriented magazines. A skiing one, maybe, and a fishing or hunting one."

"He's just bought his third TV station to add to his radio station collection."

THE TYCOON'S KISS

"He's quite the media mogul," Taylor said.

"By Montana standards," Jane answered.

"By anybody's standards. TV stations, radio stations, magazines. I think it's incredibly impressive."

"Troy helped him, you know. He gave Cormac a loan so he could buy the first couple of radio stations and then Cormac picked up the Denver-based publishing company for next to nothing a year later, and has turned the publishing company around."

Taylor clicked the binder closed and reached for *Wyoming Living*. "It'll be interesting to meet Cormac tomorrow night. I've been curious about him. I hear he's the only blond Sheenan."

"He's pretty hot... channels Channing Tatum. Some girls like that." Jane paused, flipping through the magazine. "I always liked brunettes. With blue eyes."

*Like Troy.*

Taylor's chest squeezed and she held her breath a moment. Did Jane still love Troy?

Taylor reached out, put a hand on the magazine Jane was flipping through, stopping her from turning any more pages. "We need to talk," she said quietly.

"I thought we were talking."

"About something important."

"What?"

"Are you madly in love with him?"

"Mitch? No. We've only had a couple of dates."

"Not Mitch. Troy." Taylor leaned on the counter and stared intently into Jane's face, trying to read her expression. "You're here for Troy. I've done the research. The whole wedding giveaway in 1914 was the clever brainchild of a Graff employee back in 1913, trying to figure out how to generate publicity to the reopening of the hotel after the 1912 fire." Taylor gave Jane a pointed look. "Just as you are now the clever person creating a publicity event for the new owner of the Graff Hotel."

"That's what I was hired to do, yes, but I didn't take this job for Troy. I took this job because it was an exciting opportunity and there was a big fat salary which paired nicely with Marietta's cost of living—substantially lower than San Francisco's—meaning, I could bank some money, start saving up to buy my own house."

"So you're not here to make points with Troy?"

"It doesn't hurt to make points with Troy. He knows everyone, everywhere. The man is connected."

"You love him."

"No."

"You want him back."

Jane grimaced. "No. It'd just be a waste of both our time and, to be fair to him, I knew he was never into me, but it was fun being out with Troy. Heads turned. Everyone paid attention. I felt sexy and beautiful when we were together, but I knew something was missing…. not from my side of things, but from his. He didn't feel anything. There were no sparks. I pretended not to know, or notice, but when we kissed, I could tell he didn't want to kiss me. And to be honest, it was a turn off."

"So you don't love him."

"I've been telling you that for weeks."

Taylor felt as if a massive weight tumbled from her shoulders. She breathed in, and then out, and in again, feeling lighter than she had in ages.

"I wanted him to love me," Jane added. "But apparently he felt more brotherly towards me." She slumped onto the counter. "Do you know how often I hear that? Why do men just want to be my friend?"

"You're smart. Ambitious. That's scary for men."

"Why?"

Taylor grimaced. "I don't know. Men are stupid."

Jane burst out laughing. "Did you really just say that?"

"Of course I don't mean all men, but I think men are far more insecure than they like to let on. I just don't think they've evolved as much as we woman would like to think they have."

"Are you a feminist, Taylor Harris?"

"I don't know if I'm a feminist or a realist. But I can't help thinking that men might be hampered by all their testosterone, while estrogen allows women to be flexible. Because we have to be flexible. Our lives are all about growth and contraction."

"I had no idea you were such a deep thinker."

Taylor shrugged and smiled. "Book girls rule."

Jane shook her head, smiling. "You're a nut, and for your information, I wouldn't have ever set him up with you, if I didn't think you could be the right one for him." She hesitated a moment. "Troy's liked you from the beginning."

"He didn't even know me until he scooped me up on the side of the highway."

"He knew about you long before that. Troy was a big part of you getting this job, Taylor."

"*What?*"

"Come on, you knew that. He's a board member for Marietta's Friends of the Library—"

"I did not know that. I thought Cormac was."

"Troy replaced Cormac over the summer. There was no way Cormac could care for Daisy and continue with working and holding volunteer positions on all the various non-profits, so he let most the volunteer work go."

"Wait. I'm getting confused. Daisy isn't Cormac's daughter?"

"Daisy was the daughter of Cormac's best friends, Daryl and April Wilde. Daryl and April died in that big accident on the Las Vegas strip last June. I'm sure you heard about it. The accident was all over the news. Now Cormac is raising their baby."

"Wow. I didn't know all that. And I definitely wasn't aware that Troy had been part of the hiring committee."

"He was one of the ones that recommended you."

"There were some who didn't want me?"

"There were some who thought the library should replace Margaret with someone older, and more mature."

"Like Judge McCorkle, maybe?" Taylor muttered.

Jane's eyebrows shot up. "How did you know?"

Taylor's jaw dropped. "He wasn't part of the hiring committee!"

"He was. Along with Annabeth Collier, Chelsea's mom, Sharla Dickinson, the principal at Marietta High, and Samuel Emerson of Emerson Ranch."

"Ella's dad."

Jane nodded.

"How do you know all this?" Taylor asked.

"Committee meeting notes are always saved in a city Dropbox folder I have access to as Director for the Chamber of Commerce."

"So you know Marietta's dirt."

Jane grinned. "I do."

"People should be nicer to you."

Jane laughed as she reached for her coat and purse. "Yes. Yes, they should." She slipped her coat on. "What time is Troy picking you up tomorrow night?"

"Five forty-five, so we can be there at six, since that's the start of the cocktail hour."

"I'm planning on being at the hotel by five thirty. Just to be on the safe side. Mitch is going to meet me there since I'm going so early."

"That's no fun."

"It's okay. I don't think Mitch and I have all that much in common anyway. He's a sports nut and I like the arts."

"He is a high school football coach."

"Exactly. Good looking, hunky as heck, but once again, not the right guy for me."

THAT EVENING AT home, instead of curling up with a book, Taylor gave herself a manicure and pedicure as she sat in the living room with Kara. The TV was on but Kara was reading through a huge stack of legal briefs and Taylor wasn't really paying attention to the television program.

"What color did you decide for your nails?" Kara asked, without looking up from her paperwork.

"Red."

"Good choice. So you've decided to wear the Lily Jewel gown?"

"No. Can't wear it." Taylor frowned at the smudge in her little toenail and debated redoing the nail, and then figured it was fine. No one would be looking that closely at her feet. "It's too… everything… for me. And I'd be terrified I'd tear it or spill something on it."

"She's giving it to you."

"Well, I'm giving it back. She should have someone rich and famous wear that dress. Not a boring librarian like me." Taylor screwed the cap on the nail polish, and stretched, relaxed, and happy. "I can't believe I'm saying this, but I'm

THE TYCOON'S KISS

really looking forward to tomorrow night."

"*Finally*. I've been worried about you. You have Marietta's hottest bachelor taking you to the ball. You should be counting your blessings, girl."

"I am, but not because he's Marietta's hottest bachelor, but because he's really nice. And smart. And funny. Kara, he makes me laugh and I don't think I ever laugh that much with anyone else." Taylor made a face. "I think that's what has worried me. I really do like spending time with him."

"So why is that bad?"

"Because it's not going to go anywhere. We'll attend the dance and then he'll return to San Francisco and I'll go back to my life, and I'm not calling it boring, but it's certainly not razzle dazzle and if I am being completely honestly…it's going to be hard to go back to my life the way it was. This has been fun. He's been fun. He is like Prince Charming."

Kara's expression softened. "You like him."

For a moment Taylor couldn't speak. She had fallen for Troy, just a little bit, but even that little bit was enough to make her heart ache. To make her wish that fairy tales did come true. "It's going to be fine." She glanced down at her glossy red toes and suddenly the polish blurred and she was having to blink hard to clear her eyes. "It'll take a week or two and then I'll be back in my routine."

"But first, you're going to enjoy the ball," Kara said firmly.

"*Exactly*." Taylor impatiently wiped her eyes dry, her

smile wry. "And I am going to enjoy the ball. It'll be a night to remember."

SHE WENT TO bed nervous but woke up excited. For several minutes after waking up, she just thought about the day to come and how it was so out of her norm, and yet that's also what made it so exciting. She'd had so many reservations but those were gone now and she just wanted to enjoy tonight, and she would.

Leaving bed, Taylor showered and dressed, humming show tunes. She didn't know she'd switched from humming to singing until Kara entered the kitchen and joined Taylor in the chorus from Oklahoma's *Oh What a Beautiful Morning*.

They laughed as the last note faded.

"Wow," Taylor said, reaching for her thermos of coffee, and blushing. "I don't think we've ever started the day that way."

"It was a surprise," Kara answered, grinning as she fastened her coat. "I guess you're in a good mood."

"I guess so." Taylor tucked the thermos in her tote bag. "Will I see you later this afternoon?"

"Absolutely. I want to see you all dressed. There is no way I am going to miss that."

ALL MORNING TAYLOR thought about seeing Troy that evening, and wondered if she ought to send him a text saying

THE TYCOON'S KISS

hello and that she was looking forward to seeing him. She wasn't sure if it would be appropriate, though. She also wondered if she was supposed to get him flowers...a boutonniere. But no, that's what you did for a high school dance or a wedding, not a Valentine's Ball.

At least, she hoped she was right.

At noon she ate lunch at her desk in the staff room, and was still picking at her half sandwich when she got a text from Troy.

*All good?* he texted.

*Yes*, she answered. *You?*

*Great. Just wanted to be sure you weren't getting cold feet.*

She laughed. *No cold feet,* she texted back. *See you tonight.* Hanging up, she put away the rest of her lunch and returned to work.

The rest of the afternoon passed quickly, with Taylor keeping an eye on the time since she was leaving work early to get her hair done for tonight.

Fifteen minutes before her hair appointment, Taylor grabbed her purse, coat, and said goodnight to Louise and Margaret and was heading for the door when she spotted a tall lanky body perched on the edge of the wooden bench in the drafty library foyer.

His coat was open. His dark blond hair mussed. She knew who he was immediately.

*Doug.*

Her heart fell. It was bad. Terrible. He'd broken one of the rules of his probation, leaving Hogue Ranch without permission.

Taylor hadn't even been able to speak. She just looked at him sitting on the bench, his head bent, his thin body angled forward, hands braced against his knees.

She sat down next to him. "Doug," she whispered, unable to think of anything to say. All those months at Hogue...all that time...

He didn't say a word. He just reached out and took her hand. Held it tightly.

His hand was icy cold and his fingers wrapped around hers, holding her hand snugly, desperately. She felt his pain. Felt his anger and pain and desperation.

He was in trouble. Not just trouble with Hogue, or the law, but trouble emotionally, psychologically.

"It's okay," she said.

He shook his head. His shoulders heaved. He made a rough sound deep in his chest. He was crying. Or trying not to cry. Either way, it broke her heart.

She wrapped an arm around his waist, hugged him, feeling the crisp frost on his coat. He was chilled through.

"What happened?" she asked.

He wouldn't look at her. He turned his head so she couldn't see his face. "Can't live like this. Can't continue like this."

For a second she couldn't breathe. "The depression's back?"

"It never goes."

THE TYCOON'S KISS

"Then we don't have you on the right medicine."

"I've been telling everyone that, but no one listens."

"I'm listening."

"It's too late. They'll arrest me now for leaving the ranch."

"But if you needed help, medical help—"

"It doesn't matter." He ran his hand beneath his eyes. "Doesn't change me. Doesn't change my future. Can't live like this, Taylor. I'd be better off dead."

"Well, I wouldn't. I couldn't imagine life without you." She squeezed him again, pressing as close as she could, needing to send love into him, through him, healing love, and hope. She needed hope, too. She loved her brother more than anything. Her parents might have abandoned him, but she couldn't. She wouldn't. Ever. "We just need the right doctor and the right medicine and we just have to take it one step at a time."

"I'm so sorry, Taylor. I'm so sorry for everything."

"It's not your fault. Your brain is wired differently, but it's still a beautiful brain, and you are a beautiful man and we're going to get this sorted out. I promise."

He lifted his head and looked at her. "You think?"

She inhaled as she saw his black eye and swollen nose. "What happened?"

His head dropped again. "Nothing."

Something had happened. His face was black and blue. "Who did it?"

"Doesn't matter."

"Of course, it does."

"I tried to avoid the fight. I did."

"How did it happen, and with who?"

"Doesn't matter. I left Hogue. I broke my contract. I'll be going to jail."

"Maybe. And maybe not," Taylor said, remembering what McKenna had said about hiring a good attorney. Maybe it was time to ask for favors from her friends here. McKenna knew the right people. Maybe it was time to reach out and ask for help. Brock Sheenan might be a good person to approach. The worst thing he could do was say no. "We'll go to Kara's," she added. "Make some calls, come up with a plan. Alright?"

"Who will we call tonight? Isn't that Valentine Ball taking place this evening over at the Graff?"

The ball.

*Troy.*

For a moment she'd forgotten all about tonight's ball. Remembering, made her breath catch, and her heart tumble to her feet.

She wasn't going to be able to go.

She was going to miss tonight after all.

She blinked back tears, hating herself for even feeling sorry for herself. Doug was in trouble. Doug needed her. She couldn't desert him now.

"Yes," she said. "The ball is tonight. So let's go home. Work on that plan, okay?"

# Chapter Ten

TROY WAS IN the shower in his suite at the Graff when the text arrived. He didn't notice the text until he'd finished shaving and dressing. It was while he was adjusting his tie in front of the bathroom mirror that his phone, left on the gleaming white marble counter, caught his eye.

He had a message.

He picked up the phone, checked it. It was from Taylor.

*Doug showed up at the library this afternoon. He's gotten himself into some trouble. Can't go tonight. So very sorry. Apologies!!*

He read the message a second time, disappointment washing through him.

She was bailing on him at the last minute, and yes, her brother was more important than the ball, but he'd be lying if he didn't have some mixed emotions. He told himself she wasn't rejecting him, but in light of all the ups and downs of the past week, perhaps he should have expected this.

Perhaps Taylor Harris was not the most reliable woman.

Perhaps she was so wrapped up in her brother that there wasn't time for anyone, or anything else. Or perhaps her brother was in crisis as she'd said… which meant that of course she needed to be with him.

Troy had a twin brother that was always in some sort of trouble. He knew better than any that there were some situations beyond one's control. And this was one.

His disappointment over not attending with Taylor shifted to concern for her. She probably wasn't happy at all right now. And God knows what trouble Doug had gotten himself into.

Troy frowned at his phone, wondering if he should call her. Did she need help? Was there something he could do?

Troy dragged a hand through his still damp hair before shooting her a brief response.

*Family comes first. Do what you have to do and don't worry about me. But are you okay? Do you need anything?*

He hit send on the text and slipped his phone into the pocket of his black tuxedo trousers and went to work styling his hair and giving his tie one last little tweak.

He still needed to slip on his jacket, but he looked alright. Shouldn't embarrass himself or anyone else tonight.

He was perfectly fine going to the ball solo. And it's not as if Taylor was the only one to cancel on the Valentine Ball at the last minute. Dillon had decided to stay home with Dad. And out in California Daisy had a violent stomach bug

THE TYCOON'S KISS

so Cormac chose to stay with her instead of getting on a plane for Marietta.

He respected both Dillon and Cormac for making good choices. And if Taylor's brother, Doug, was in trouble, then she was doing the right thing, staying home with him.

Fortunately, Brock and Harley were still joining him at the Sheenan table, and Jane and Mitch would be there, too. So what if it was now a table of five instead of ten? Sheenans liked having some elbow room.

TAYLOR READ THE text from Troy and it was a very nice text from him. He'd said exactly the right thing, behaved as a gentleman should, but it didn't make her feel better.

She didn't want to miss the ball.

She didn't want to sit and watch TV with Doug, or order a pizza as Kara had suggested. But that's what she was going to do, because it was the right thing to do.

Kara disagreed. She thought Taylor should still go, and she reminded Taylor that she was at the house tonight, wrapping up some work stuff so she could take off next week to go skiing with friends from law school without worrying about anything. "I'm here," Kara said. "I'll keep him company. We'll have pizza—"

"I've already told Troy I'm not going."

Until that moment, Doug hadn't any idea that Taylor had been invited to the big ball and he was upset that Taylor was missing the event because of him.

"Why don't you go?" he asked Taylor, joining his sister and Kara in the kitchen where they'd been trying to decide on what pizza to order. "It's still early. You can make it."

"It's fine—"

"It's not," he interrupted. "It's bad enough I screwed up my probation but I don't need to screw up your life, too."

"You're not screwing it up."

"All I've ever done is screw it up." He leaned against the counter and dug his hands into his jeans pockets. "Taylor, I'm not going to go anywhere tonight. I'm not going to do anything bad. I'm going to eat pizza and watch TV and crash early. I'm tired. But I'm not dangerous. I'm not psycho. Not a flight risk. I'm not going to do anything stupid tonight. I've done enough, walking out of Hogue. I know I'm in trouble."

"I don't think you're in as much trouble as you think," Kara said. "We'll take some pictures tonight of your black eye and bruises, and tomorrow if need be, Taylor can take you to a doctor and get a medical exam. The photos and exam will serve as evidence that Hogue isn't protecting you, and that you're in danger there. I'm not able to represent you, but Doug, in my opinion, if you're getting beat up at Hogue, you need to leave, and you have grounds to leave. We just need the right attorney and we're going to work this out."

Doug glanced at Taylor and back to Kara. "You really think so?"

THE TYCOON'S KISS

"Hogue was never the right place for you," Kara said. "And it's time we sorted this out, once and for all." She gave Taylor a look. "And you… you really should go to the ball. If you stay home tonight, Doug's just going to worry and feel guilty, and responsible, and there's no reason for that. There's no reason for you *not* to go. Get dressed, do your hair and drive over. Surprise Troy."

"Surprise Troy," Taylor repeated.

Kara nodded. "Live a little."

"Or live a lot," Doug added with a lopsided smile.

Taylor looked at her brother, saw his hopeful expression and felt the warmth steal back into her heart. Maybe they were right. Maybe it was time she lived.

*A lot.*

A HALF HOUR later Taylor stared at her reflection in the bathroom mirror.

Her breath caught in her throat as she gently touched the skirt of her pale pink tulle gown, the tulle dotted with glossy red spangles. She watched herself in the mirror as she lightly ran her hand up the gown's fitted, boned bodice to the plunging neckline.

The ball gown pushed her breasts up, squeezed her waist smaller, and shaped her hips, revealing far more of her slender frame than Taylor was normally comfortable with, because good librarians didn't show off their breasts, or flaunt their hips, or draw attention to any other part of their bodies.

But tonight Taylor didn't want to be a good librarian.

Tonight she didn't want to be a librarian at all. She didn't want to be the smart one, or the good one, or the responsible one who was always rescuing, protecting and defending her brother.

No, tonight, for one night, she'd be someone else. She'd be someone different, someone beautiful and glamorous and fun, and she'd go to the Valentine Ball at the Graff Hotel and have fun.

She wasn't even sure what fun felt like, but she knew that whenever she was with Troy she felt good.

She felt happy.

That's the feeling she wanted tonight. Good and happy.

A knock sounded on the bathroom door. Taylor opened the door and faced Kara. "What do you think?" she asked shyly.

Kara's eyes opened wide. "You're wearing the Lily Jewel gown."

"You said I should live a little." Taylor lightly stroked her fingers across the full skirt with the circle spangles. "I feel like a walking carnival or circus."

"You look gorgeous."

"It's the dress."

"It's *you*, in the *dress*." Kara walked around Taylor to inspect her properly. "I love that you're also wearing your hair up. Very chic."

THE TYCOON'S KISS

"There was no time to get a blow out."

"Looks good." Kara tilted her head to the side. "What about earrings?"

"I have my diamond studs."

"Those will work. And your make up looks good. I love the eyeliner and mascara, too."

"Thought I'd better wear more make up since I've got my contacts in."

"You're a knock out."

"No—"

"Yes," Kara insisted. "Poor Troy. He isn't going to know what hit him."

IT WAS ALMOST seven by the time Taylor reached the hotel, and snowing. Taylor parked her car as close to the hotel entrance as she could manage, and held her full skirts up to keep them from dragging in the snow and ice.

Entering the hotel's grand lobby with the marble floor and tall columns and rich dark paneling, Taylor felt her heart skip a beat.

She felt like a princess attending her first ball. It was exciting. Thrilling. And she did feel pretty tonight, truly pretty, and that never happened. Normally she felt smart, practical, helpful, *useful*. Not lovely or delicate, and certainly not ridiculously feminine.

But her gown was ridiculously feminine with the dotting of red spangles that reflected light, making her feel like a valentine that had come to life.

She couldn't wait to check her coat and enter the ball-room. She wanted everyone to see her gorgeous dress and most of all, she wanted Troy to see her in this dress.

He said Lily Jewel had 'given' her the dress, but Taylor knew that gifts like that didn't just happen. Troy orchestrated the gift. Taylor wasn't sure what he said or did and right now it didn't matter. All that mattered was that she would soon be attending her first ball with the most handsome man she'd ever met.

Even though it was almost seven, lots of people were still arriving and the entry hall outside the hotel's grand ballroom echoed with laughter and chatter as couples arrived for the Valentine Ball, and checked their coats and greeted each other.

Taylor handed over her winter coat and then shivered as she stepped away from the coat room, feeling almost naked in the strapless gown.

But she wasn't naked, she was a walking valentine... light, lovely, delicious.

She wasn't going to allow herself to feel one negative emotion, either. She wasn't going to let herself feel doubt or fear.

No, tonight was a celebration, of not just one thing, but many things—the restoration of the historic Graff Hotel, the launch of the 100 year anniversary of the Great Wedding Giveaway, and the intrepid individual who dared to take risks, and dream.

TROY SAW HER enter the ballroom, passing through the tall double doors alone, and then hesitate in the doorway, her ball gown gleaming in the pink lighting, a clutch pressed to her chest, her dark hair pulled up in an elegant chignon, reminding him of a young Audrey Hepburn.

Striking features, and wide bright eyes. No glasses tonight. She'd left them home.

She scanned the ballroom.

He pretended he didn't know her and imagined the man she was looking for—her boyfriend or lover. Not her husband.

It wasn't that she was too young to be married—many women in Montana married young, choosing their high school or college sweethearts—but she didn't have a married look. She didn't appear settled, although he wasn't entirely sure what settled would look like, but married women carried themselves differently. They had a different confidence about them—perhaps it was complacency—that young, unmarried women didn't have.

Either way, in the doorway, she was truly lovely, and in that moment he realized she wasn't merely pretty, but beautiful, and delicate, in her romantic ball gown with the sweetheart bodice.

Troy walked towards her, wondering how she'd managed to sneak away from the house to be here, hoping she didn't regret doing so, either. He was so happy to see her. So glad she'd come after all.

There was no other woman he'd rather be with tonight.

But then, from the heavy staccato within his chest, and the silver heat in his veins, he suspected that there was no other woman he'd rather be with, any night.

"Taylor," he said, reaching her side.

Her head turned sharply and she looked at him, smiling. "Hello, Troy," she said, her voice soft, light. Even her dark eyes were so full of light they sparkled. "You look very dashing tonight."

"And you look stunning, my lady. You are the belle of the ball."

"I hope you still need a date. Please tell me you haven't replaced me."

"I could never replace you."

"So full of flattery."

"I am speaking the absolute truth. There is only one Taylor Harris and I very much want her."

She blushed. "Why?"

"I have a secret soft spot for book girls. I happen to think you book girls are very cool."

Her eyes lit up and her lips curved. "I've always said the same thing."

"As you should." He offered her his arm. "Shall we find a glass of champagne and then locate our table? Dinner is about to be served."

THE TYCOON'S KISS

"I've been in California since I left for college at eighteen. I went to Stanford University in Palo Alto."

"You studied?"

"Electrical engineering and computer science."

"So computer science was your minor?"

"I was a double major, and then a graduate degree in the same."

She eyed him with new respect. "You are smart."

He grinned. "I am more than just a pretty face."

She laughed. "I can't believe you just said that."

"It was a calculated move on my part. I wanted to make you laugh, and I succeeded." He reached for a candied walnut and popped it in his mouth. "So what do you like better? My brains or my beauty?"

Taylor loved the glint in his eye and the hint of mischief in his smile. "Your sense of humor." She sipped her champagne, enjoying the cold tart fizz in her mouth and the way the bubbles warmed her going down. "Tell me about the girlfriend."

"Which one? There have been many."

"The last. And why have there been so many?"

"So many questions."

"I'm curious about you. And the women you love." She took another quick sip of champagne. "And leave."

One of his black brows lifted. "I'm not out to break hearts. I'm just not going to settle."

"So what was wrong with the last one?"

"There's not much to say. She was a lovely woman. We dated for a number of months, but it wasn't a forever relationship. It couldn't go the distance."

"Why not?"

"We had different values and goals, as well as a different vision for the future." He saw her expression and shrugged. "She couldn't understand my love affair with the Graff. She came from money. Her family is old money in San Francisco, and big philanthropists, but she doesn't believe in rescuing decrepit buildings in the middle of nowhere. She believed my money would have been better spent funding a museum or donating to the San Francisco arts."

"That's why you broke up?"

"There were other issues, fundamental issues about identity, integrity, and loyalty, and I appreciate that her family is a well-known family, and I appreciate that she is an heiress in her own right, but I'm not jumping through hoops for anybody. I am who I am, and that's a Sheenan, from Marietta, Montana. I don't come from big money, and I don't care what others think of me. I don't want a woman that cares more about society's opinion than mine. I want a woman who is herself and has a strong sense of self, because our relationship has to be based on mutual respect, not status or public adulation."

"Was she beautiful?"

Troy suddenly closed the distance between them, kissing her lightly on the lips. "You are more beautiful." He kissed her again. "And smarter." His fingers brushed her cheek, his thumb stroking over the sweep of her cheekbone before kissing her a third time. "And one hundred times more intriguing. Any more questions?"

She stared into his deep blue eyes, lost. In the back of her mind she was sure there were more questions, dozens of them, but her head was spinning and her heart was racing and she just wanted to go somewhere private and kiss some more. "No," she murmured. "At least, no more right now."

THE NIGHT JUST got better from there.

Dinner was wonderful and Taylor talked to Harley and Brock, Jane and Mitch, aware of Troy's arm resting lightly along the back of her chair. Now and then his hand would move to her back, and he'd touch her, a soft caress to the middle of her back, a light touch at her nape and she'd tingle and burn.

It didn't feel like a first date or a Valentine Ball. Being with him was exciting and yet somehow familiar. She was strangely comfortable with him. Had they known each other perhaps in a different life?

Taylor darted a glance at him as Jane and Mitch headed off to the dance floor.

Troy smiled at her. "Yes?"

"Just wondering if you were doing okay."

The corner of his mouth tugged. "I'm alright. And you?"

"I'm alright, too."

He lifted her hand, carried it to his mouth and kissed her palm. "Do you want to dance?"

"Not if you don't."

"I'm happy being with you. Don't care if it's here, or on the dance floor—" he broke off as Taylor stiffened. "What's wrong?"

"Judge McCorkle," she whispered, nodding at the couple approaching. "I don't like him."

Troy looked from the judge and his wife to Taylor. "Why not?"

"It's... personal."

"Did he say something to you?"

"I'll tell you later."

There was no time to say anything else as Judge McCorkle and his wife were upon them. Troy rose, and Taylor more reluctantly. The judge ignored her but greeted Troy effusively.

It was Troy who introduced Taylor to Mrs. McCorkle. "Sarah, I don't know if you've met Taylor Harris."

"No, I haven't," Sarah McCorkle answered. "It's a pleasure to meet you."

"She's the new librarian," the judge boomed.

"Yes, I know," his wife answered.

"How is your brother?" the judge asked, fixing his narrowed gaze on Taylor. "Staying out of trouble?"

Taylor squared her shoulders and lifted her chin. "How thoughtful of you to remember him." She smiled at the

THE TYCOON'S KISS

judge, a wide dazzling smile, thinking she'd kill him with kindness. "I will be sure to let Doug know you asked about him."

And then Troy saved her, wrapping his arm around her and squeezing her close. "If you'll excuse us, this is our song. We have to dance."

"Now?" The judge said frowning.

"Yeah, now." Troy kissed the top of Taylor's head. "You remember how it was when you fell in love. You'd do anything for your girl." And then Troy took her hand and, with their fingers laced, drew her after him onto the crowded dance floor.

It was a slow song and when Troy found a spot for them he pulled her into his arms. "You don't like Judge McCorkle," he said, settling a hand low on her back.

She shivered at the touch, thinking it was delicious to be held so securely. "No," she said, tipping her head back to better see Troy's face. "And I appreciate you standing up for me, but you didn't have to tell him we were in love—"

"You don't think it's going to happen?"

She felt herself flush, color sweeping up her chest into her cheeks, making them burn. "This is pretty much a first date."

"We've been having first dates all week."

"We barely know each other."

"Is this your way of telling me you're not a fan?"

She laughed because Troy—staggeringly good looking as

183

well as smart and loyal and funny—was absolutely swoon worthy. How could she not be a fan? "I just think you're very optimistic for a bachelor that has managed to remain a bachelor for thirty-some years."

"Maybe it's because I was holding out for the right girl."

She blushed again, and didn't know where to look. "You're a flirt."

"Not flirting, *wooing*." He smiled lazily down at her, his blue gaze glinting. "There is a difference. Shall I spell it out?"

"Are we using dictionary definitions, Mr. Sheenan?"

"Absolutely. I intend to use the Merriam-Webster dictionary definition if that meets with your approval."

She struggled to hold back a laugh. "The Merriam-Webster is an approved resource."

"Thank you, Miss Harris." His head dipped and his lips brushed her temple and then her cheek, traveling ever so lightly to the curve of her ear. "Flirting is to behave in a way that shows sexual attraction but is not to be taken seriously."

His warm breath at her ear and the pitch of his deep voice made her tingle. Her fingers curled around his neck. "And wooing?" she whispered.

"To woo is to try to make someone love you." He drew back to look her in the eyes. "To try to have a romantic relationship. Which is what I'd like to have with you."

He'd just thrown the "L" word around again. As well as the "R" word. Love. Relationships. What was the world coming to?

THE TYCOON'S KISS

"You're smiling," he said, but he was smiling, too.

"I am." Her heart was doing a mad staccato as well. "I'm also not sure what to think. You're very bold."

His lips twitched. "Absolutely brazen."

"Is this how you get women into bed?"

"No. I just take off my shirt for that. You, my dear, require a plan."

"A bold one," she teased.

"Brazen," he agreed.

"Why so much effort?"

"Because you're a keeper." He gazed down at her. "Any other objections right now? Because as much as I enjoy conversation, I'd really rather kiss you right now."

He was still holding her gaze and she was lost in his blue eyes. He was magnificent. A fairy-tale prince at a fairy-tale ball. "This doesn't make sense," she said.

"But when has life ever made sense?"

## Chapter Eleven

A HALF HOUR later Troy and Taylor wound their way through the crowded dance floor back to their table.

Taylor was breathless as she sat back down in her seat. Troy had loosened his black tie. His cheekbones had a lovely dusky color. He was so incredible. Handsome, witty, kind, sexy...He should be out of her league. He was out of her league.

And yet she felt comfortable with him, at ease in a way she couldn't have imagined just a few days ago. Was it because of what he said...that he wanted to woo, not flirt? Or, was it the energy between them was warm and exciting in the best sort of way?

Because dancing with him, kissing him made her feel good, and beautiful. She'd never felt so beautiful in her life and it wasn't just her gorgeous gown or her hair or being here in this ballroom, it was the way he looked at her. The smile in his eyes, and the curve of his lips.

He made her feel truly special. Valuable. And that was a

THE TYCOON'S KISS

heady feeling. It was such a really, truly lovely feeling that she wasn't going to question this, or him anymore tonight. She wanted to savor the evening. She wanted to glory in the chemistry and the bright, electric sparks zinging through her.

Maybe Troy wasn't out of her league.

Maybe Troy was exactly her type.

"You look happy," Troy said, filling her water glass and then his.

"I am." Her heart was thumping and it wasn't just because they'd been dancing like crazed people on the dance floor.

"You had fun out there?" he asked, handing her a glass.

"I did." She smiled at him. "You're quite good out there. You have serious moves."

"I don't think you get out much."

Taylor laughed. "I think you know I tend to spend most nights home, with my books."

"And yet here you are, the belle of the ball."

"I'm not sure I'm the belle, but I am grateful to you for making this possible." She lifted her water glass, and held it up in a toast. "To you, Troy, for getting me out and making sure tonight was great fun."

He clinked his water glass to hers. "And to you, for being such great company. I'm a fan, Taylor Harris. Of you, your laugh, your passion for books, and your intriguing bright mind."

A waiter materialized with a tray and champagne but

Taylor shook her head. "I think I've had enough."

Troy refused the drink, too. "I'm good," he said, before asking, "Are you always careful with what you drink?"

She nodded. "I'm painfully responsible."

"So what is your limit?"

"Two if I've a ride, or zero if I'm driving. I just couldn't live with myself if I made a mistake...hurt someone else because I had to have a good time."

He smoothed a loose tendril back from her cheek, and studied her face, his gaze lingering on her lips. "I'm beginning to think you're perfect, Miss Harris."

"Not perfect," she said softly. "Far from perfect. There is so much about me you wouldn't like."

"Try me."

"I'm not a city girl."

"Why would that be a negative?"

"You love big cities."

"And small towns, and I like this small town girl very much. So what else?"

"I worry a lot."

"Because you have a big heart."

"I don't always compartmentalize well."

"That comes with time and experience."

Her chest squeezed, tender. "You know all the right things to say."

"I don't know about that, but I do have a feeling you tend to be hard on yourself, and you expect a lot from

THE TYCOON'S KISS

yourself. Maybe too much." His blue gaze held hers. "It's not a weakness to ask for help, or to accept help."

She didn't know what to say and the silence stretched. And Troy just waited, lifting a black brow, his expression quizzical, maybe even gently mocking because she knew he wasn't trying to hurt her, but help, and she did appreciate it. In fact, it might have been the kindest most wonderful compliment he could pay her...that he liked her enough to want to help her.

"You're used to being independent, and I respect that," he added after a moment. "But it's okay to let others help you now and then."

She struggled to smile around the lump in her throat. Truly it was getting hard to breathe and the lump wasn't getting smaller, either. "I'll keep that in mind should I ever need help."

"I think you could use some help now." He leaned in, expression intent. "McKenna told me to ask you about Judge McCorkle—"

"No. Troy, no."

"And I was going to, after the ball, but I heard what he said to you tonight, about Doug—"

"I wish you hadn't heard that."

"I don't know the whole story but I want you to tell me."

"This isn't your problem, or your mess. It's mine. And Doug is my responsibility. I won't let him be a burden for anyone else—"

"He's not a burden. He's your brother. And he's young. Just a boy."

His words undid her. They were exactly the right words. Her eyes filled with tears and she had to reach up to dash them away before they could fall. "I can't cry," she whispered. "Tonight is supposed to be special."

"It is special. You are special, and I can't ignore the fact that Judge McCorkle has really upset you. I need to understand what's happened. So let's go talk, somewhere private."

SOMEWHERE PRIVATE TURNED out to be the luxurious owner's suite on the fourth floor of the Graff.

Taylor suddenly got nervous as they stepped out of the brass elevators into the quiet hallway.

"Is this your bachelor lair?" she asked, trying to be light and funny as he unlocked the door, trying to hide that she'd lost her confidence.

"Is it my man cave when I'm in town? Yes. Do I bring women here? No." He flicked on lights and shut the door behind her. "You're the first."

That caught her off guard and she looked up at him, surprised. "Really?"

He shrugged, looking almost embarrassed. "Will it disappoint you to know that I'm not much of a man-whore?"

She couldn't stifle the gurgle of laughter. "I don't think I ever thought of you as a man-whore. Maybe a bit of a playboy, and that's only because you're handsome and charming and wildly successful."

He opened the small refrigerator in the suite's sleek kitchen and glanced inside. "Still water, mineral water, fruity bubbly water, white wine…?" He glanced at her over his shoulder. "Anything sound good?"

"I'll do a bubbly fruity water."

He drew out the glass bottles and unscrewed the caps. "Want a glass?" he asked.

"I'm fine with the bottle."

"Me, too." He led the way into the living room and took a seat on the big cream sectional. Taking a seat he patted to the cushion next to him. "Come, sit. Fill me in. On all of it. From the beginning."

She grimaced. "That could take all night."

"I have nowhere to go."

"Well, I should be home before dawn."

"Then you shall be. But that gives us, uh—" he shook his wrist, and glanced at his watch. "Six to seven hours."

Taylor's pulse was beating a little too hard, too fast. She took a gulp of her fruity bubbly water and then told him everything, starting with how Doug had battled depression since he was in high school—probably even before that—but she recognized his struggles in high school and knew he needed clinical help.

She told him how their parents didn't think he had depression, because they didn't believe in depression and her father just thought Doug was lazy and self-indulgent. She told him she'd been the one to get him to a doctor and how it took awhile to find the right medicine, but that after awhile sometimes the right medicine stopped working, and that sometimes he needed a new dose, or something else added in. She told him about the day when Doug got pulled over for speeding and how Doug hadn't been properly respectful and the sheriff arrested Doug. From there, everything just went downhill fast. Judge McCorkle came down hard on Doug, and sentenced him to six months at Hogue, and then instead of letting him finish his probation at home with her, the judge said Doug had to stay at the ranch for another six months.

Taylor wiped away tears as she talked. She hated crying and didn't want to cry now. She wasn't looking for pity or help. But it was impossible to talk about Doug, and how he'd been treated by Judge McCorkle without feeling fury and frustration.

"My brother is a good person," she said, voice cracking. "And yes, he struggles, but that doesn't make him a bad person. It just means he's human. But instead of Judge McCorkle having any compassion, he's determined to punish Doug for having a mood disorder. It makes me so angry. So so angry." She knocked away another tear. "That's why I don't talk about it. Not because I'm ashamed, but because I'm heartsick. Absolutely heartsick. Judge McCorkle is ignorant and his ignorance is hurting others and they're suffering enough without his contempt—"

She broke off, looked away. She shook her head, regretting saying so much.

She'd learned long ago it was better to not say what you really felt because people didn't want to know what you really felt. They didn't want truth, especially if the truth was uncomfortable. Her parents had taught her that, and so had teachers and employers. Never mind Judge McCorkle.

And Taylor did try to be pleasant and agreeable. She was determined to keep things light most of the time, but it wasn't easy smashing all those strong feelings down, suppressing all her emotions. That's why she disappeared into her books so often. Books let her think and feel. When she read it was okay to feel intensely, and okay to want things and need things…okay to be angry with people who had let you down, okay to be disappointed that so many people were afraid of complex situations.

But life was complex. And complicated. People were complicated, too.

"I'm sorry," she said when she could trust herself to speak more calmly. "I'm sorry for getting so upset. I'm sure I made you uncomfortable—"

"You didn't," he said quietly.

"It's so hard to talk about."

"For good reason. You love your brother and he's suffering, and so you're suffering, too."

She looked at him, struggled to smile, wanting him to know she was grateful for understanding, but he didn't yet know all of it. He didn't know that Doug had walked away from the Hogue and once the judge found out it'd be even worse. "Remember how I texted you earlier that Doug had showed up at the library today? Well, you're not allowed to leave the ranch, and Doug did, which meant he broke his probation and so he'll be back in court and Judge McCorkle will lose his mind. But Troy, Doug can't go back to that ranch. It's not a good place for him, not a good fit. If you saw Doug you'd see what I'm talking about. He's got bruises everywhere. His face is a mess—" she broke off, gulped a breath. "He's not a fighter. He's never been a fighter. That's just not who he is."

"He was beat up?"

She nodded.

"And Kara knows?" he asked.

She nodded again. "She's staying with him tonight."

"What does she say about all of this?"

"She said that we need a good attorney, and that a good attorney could prove that the Hogue isn't protecting Doug and help us sort things out once and for all."

"If Kara thinks you need to hire an attorney, then hire an attorney, because she wouldn't give you bad advice. She knows what she's talking about."

"I'm going to do it."

For a long moment Troy said nothing. He sat there, staring off in the distance, his hand running over his jaw, rubbing at the bristles. "Why didn't you hire someone before?"

Taylor glanced at him, took in his hard jaw and stern expression and realized that although he was gentle with her, he was not a pushover. "Every good attorney requires a retainer. I don't just have thousands sitting in a bank account."

"You have a job."

"Yes, but I also have bills and loans and Doug's medicine. It's not covered by my insurance and it is hundreds of dollars every month."

"Why isn't it covered by insurance?"

She shifted uncomfortably. "Because he doesn't have insurance that will cover mental health stuff. It's one of those chicken and the egg things."

"Your parents don't help support him?"

"No."

"Do you get any financial assistance from anywhere for him?"

She shook her head.

Troy was looking at her now, studying her, his dark blue gaze intent. "You're a good sister."

"He's my world."

"That's what I mean. You are a good sister. And a very beautiful person, inside and out."

She blinked, determined not to cry again tonight, but touched by the compliment. "Thank you."

He was still looking at her, really looking at her, seeing

her, and it kind of stole her breath, the way he was looking at her...

He liked her. Really liked *her*. She could feel it, see it.

"We should thank Jane," he said.

She smiled tremulously. "Yes."

The words died away and for a long moment there was just silence. The kind of silence that hummed and shimmered with all the things that words couldn't communicate.

Hope, hunger, heat, desire.

Troy leaned forward, and drew her towards him, closing the distance. "I've been dying to do this ever since I got you in here," he murmured, pulling her onto his lap. "It's been hard keeping my hands off of you."

Her heart did a funny little beat. "Even though I was a sobbing wreck?"

"You weren't a wreck." He brushed his lips across hers, sending shooting sparks up and down her spine. "But you did have a good cry."

She smiled against his mouth. "Where is my mascara now?"

"Um, on your chin."

She laughed softly and dragged her mouth across his, loving the hot sparks that shot through her veins. "As long as they're not on my dress. It's a very expensive dress."

"I'd say maybe we should take the dress off, but if that happens things would most definitely happen, and I don't think you're ready for that. I want to take this slow for you.

THE TYCOON'S KISS

Let your head catch up with your heart."

"What does that mean?"

"I think the romantic you believes in love at first sight and all that wonderful fizzy stuff, but the practical survivor you is mistrustful of love and happy-endings so you're going to struggle with this, with *us*, for awhile."

"Is there an us?" she asked.

"Yes. Most definitely."

Smiling, she reached up to lightly drag her nails down his cheek. He felt good. So good. And so real. She wanted to kiss him. And more. "I'm not good at this stuff," she whispered.

"It's just you and me, baby."

Her heart did a painful double beat. "I'm afraid I'll get this part wrong. I'm not a big city girl—"

"Haven't we covered this one already? I don't want a big city girl, and I'm not a big city guy. I just want you. I like you. Can't you tell?"

And then he was kissing her, showing her how much he liked her and they kissed until they were both a little frenzied but her gorgeous gown stayed on, as did his tuxedo and eventually they fell asleep where they were on the couch, wrapped in each other's arms.

Taylor woke up sometime in the night and yawning she lifted her head, looked at Troy who was still asleep.

He looked so much younger asleep. He looked...almost sweet...but also still so very appealing and sexy.

It had been years since she'd done this and she felt some

of the same shyness the first time she'd slept next to a man. Men were such different creatures. Big and hard on the outside and yet surprisingly tender on the inside.

Exhaling slowly, she closed her eyes and tried to relax and fall back asleep but it was hard to sleep when so many different emotions raced through her, making her insides feel raw and tender.

A week ago she would have never thought this was possible. Even two days ago she wouldn't have thought this was possible…

Now look at her… wrapped in Troy's arms, falling for him, hard. So hard.

And yet somehow it felt right. Him, her, together…

Everything worked. *They* worked. She didn't know how, didn't know why, but maybe she didn't have to have all the answers. Maybe it was enough to just feel wonderful.

Maybe Troy was right, maybe there was an *us*.

Taylor must have fallen back asleep because the next thing she knew Troy was waking her with a kiss. "Hey Sleeping Beauty," he murmured, his deep voice raspy. "It's almost six. We better get you home. Don't want to worry Kara or Doug."

MARIETTA WAS STILL dark when Troy drove the five blocks from the hotel to Kara's house on Bramble. The small yellow house was dark when Troy pulled up in front of it and turned off the engine.

THE TYCOON'S KISS

"You didn't need to drive me home," she repeated.

"I didn't trust the icy roads. It is bad out there."

"You don't trust me, or the roads?" she teased, leaning over to kiss him goodbye.

"You're not getting rid of me yet," he said, growling. "I'll walk you to the door."

She laughed softly. "You sound like a caveman."

But moments later she was grateful he was there as she stepped from his SUV. Her high heel hit a patch of ice on the sidewalk and she would have gone down hard if Troy hadn't steadied her. "That could have been ugly," she said.

"You're determined to wreck the dress. Poor Lily Jewel."

She laughed through chattering teeth as he walked her to the door. On the porch she dug through her little purse for her keys. "Now you see why I don't wear expensive clothes."

She was just about to unlock the front door when it suddenly swung open. Doug was on the other side, in the shadowy hall, and he looked even worse this morning than he had yesterday. His eye was swollen shut, and purple and yellow bruises covered his face.

"Did I wake you?" she asked him, looking away from his face to focus on putting the keys back in her purse. She knew he wasn't a little boy anymore but it didn't make seeing him this way any easier.

"I've been up for a couple hours."

"Couldn't sleep?"

"Was worried about you."

"That's my fault," Troy said, stepping forward. He put out his hand and introduced himself to Doug. "I'm Troy Sheenan. You must be Doug."

Doug glanced from Troy back to Taylor, then he shook Troy's hand. "Nice to meet you, Mr. Sheenan."

"Call me Troy."

"Yes, sir."

Troy's mouth quirked. "I am sorry for keeping your sister out all night. Should have let you know. You're a good brother to be concerned."

Doug's expression was shuttered. He seemed to be sizing Troy up, trying to decide if he liked him or not. Finally he shrugged. "As long as she's safe, and had a good time."

Taylor smiled, relieved. "It was an amazing party. I had such a good time." She gave her brother a quick hug. "And I should have texted you, Doug, and let you know everything was fine—"

"It's fine," he interrupted gruffly. "I'm not your dad and you're an adult." He flicked on the porch light and then the hall light. "Do you want coffee? I just made a big pot."

"I'd love some," Taylor said. "Troy?"

But Troy shook his head. "I should get home and give Dillon a break. He's been with Dad twenty-four hours straight and he'll want to get out and have some free time before I return to California."

Taylor's heart fell. "When do you go back?"

"Tomorrow morning." He glanced at Doug. "It was

# THE TYCOON'S KISS

good to meet you, Doug. I hope I have the chance to get to know you better." And then Troy was gone, heading down the walkway to his big black SUV. Taylor watched until he reached the truck and then carefully closed the front door.

She was home, she thought as she followed Doug into the kitchen for a much needed cup of coffee. Home and back to reality.

She doctored her coffee with creamer and sweetener and tried to focus on Doug who was telling her about the movie he'd watched last night with Kara, but it was hard to concentrate on the plot twists in the film when she couldn't stop thinking about her life.

The Valentine's Ball was over. Troy was returning to San Francisco. Was the fairy tale over, too? Or could there possibly be another chapter...?

## Chapter Twelve

AFTER LUNCH, KARA offered to drive Taylor to pick up her car from the hotel since it'd warmed up and the roads would be more slushy than icy.

But Taylor glanced out at the bright blue sky and shook her head, refusing the offer. "I'll just walk. I can use the exercise."

Doug overheard the exchange and left the TV room to join them in the kitchen. "I'll go with you, Tay. It'd be great to get out. I'm kind of going a little bit crazy here, all cooped up."

"I'd love company," Taylor said. "But do you have anything warm to wear?"

"He can wear one of my dad's coats," Kara offered, aware that all of Doug's things were still at Hogue. "And I'm sure there are tons of extra scarves and hats and gloves in the closet, too. Just dig around, find something that fits."

While Doug looked for something that would fit, Kara asked Taylor about the ball. "So…anything juicy to share?

Did you have fun? Was he any good? Did you sleep at all…?"

Taylor smothered yet another yawn, very much in need of a nap. "I did sleep, for a couple hours. And no, we didn't have sex." She saw Kara's dubious expression. "We talked a lot and then kissed for hours. He is a very good kisser."

"I guess that's good."

Taylor made a face. "You should be glad that he respected me."

"Right. And I am. That's super romantic."

Taylor rolled her eyes. "It was practically our first date."

Now it was Kara's turn to roll her eyes. "You guys have talked and texted all week. Stop acting like you're strangers, or virgins—" she broke off, eyes widening. "You're not a virgin, are you?"

"*No.*" Taylor took her coat off the peg by the kitchen door. "But it has been a long, long time." She saw Kara's expression and grimaced. "Technically, I am not. Emotionally, I could be. But can we not talk about this anymore? It's mortifying."

AFTER GETTING THE car Taylor and Doug decided to go see a movie and then get dinner at the Chinese restaurant next door to the theater on Front Street. They swung by the grocery store on the way home so Taylor could pick up something to make for dinner tomorrow and let Doug buy a new toothbrush and razor and shaving cream.

Kara was out when they reached the house, but a giant red glass vase of lush roses and tulips sat on the front porch. It wasn't a cheap arrangement by any means. Grabbing the bag of groceries, Doug headed for the porch. He picked up the flowers and checked the name on the envelope. "It's for you, Tay."

Her heart did a quick beat and she immediately thought of Troy. Was it from him? Had he come by himself to drop off the flowers?

In the house she opened the envelope. *For my favorite Book Girl. Happy Valentine's Day. Troy*

"Is it from him?" Doug asked. "Mr. Sheenan?"

She nodded and read the message on the card again.

"That's nice of him," he said.

She nodded again and put the card away. It was nice of Troy. The only thing nicer would have been seeing him in person. Maybe tomorrow she could meet him for coffee before he left.

Taylor grabbed her phone and shot him a quick text. *Thank you for the flowers. They're beautiful.*

Troy didn't answer right away and for the next couple of hours she checked her phone and rechecked it waiting for a reply. She finally got one just before midnight.

*Just landed in San Jose. Had to return for an emergency meeting. Glad you like the flowers. I'll be in touch soon.*

Taylor put her phone back down on her nightstand but couldn't fall back asleep.

THE TYCOON'S KISS

He'd left. He was back in California. Gone.

She wasn't going to see him tomorrow. She couldn't grab coffee and chat. He'd jumped in his plane and flown away and now that he was halfway across the country, she didn't know when he'd be back.

HE DIDN'T CALL on Sunday. He didn't text, either. Nor did she hear from him on Monday and it crossed Taylor's mind as she dressed for work Tuesday that maybe, just maybe, she'd read too much into Troy's attention, and that maybe just maybe he'd been kind and attentive and an excellent date, but he wasn't ready for more. That his idea of a relationship wasn't hers.

Or maybe he'd never wanted a relationship and he had just been flirting.

Maybe it had all been lines, smooth lines to wrap her around his finger.

She went to Java Café for lunch Tuesday, needing to get out for a bit since she'd be working late, meeting with the Tuesday Night Book Club. She did not love meeting with the Tuesday Night Book Club.

Taylor was trudging back to the library following lunch when her phone rang. She didn't recognize the number, but answered, aware that Doug's court date had been scheduled for the end of the week and she was waiting to hear back from a lawyer.

It wasn't the lawyer, though. It was Kara calling from her

office, using the office line instead of her cell. "Taylor, you didn't hear this from me but I had to tell you that I've just learned that Judge McCorkle is going to allow Doug to finish his probation at home, with you. There will be no additional charges. Doug won't have to go to court on Friday. It's all over. As long as Doug doesn't get into trouble in the next few months, it's done."

"What do you mean, it's done?"

"Judge McCorkle has agreed to let Doug remain with you. He does not have to return to Hogue. He just needs to remain with you and meet the terms of his probation, but that shouldn't be a problem, should it?"

"No." Taylor was shocked and thrilled. She couldn't wait to tell Doug. They could get his things from Hogue and he never had to deal with that place again. What a relief. It was wonderful news. But she knew someone had to have pulled some strings and she was sure it was Troy. "Was Troy behind this?"

"I don't know for sure," Kara answered honestly, "but I wouldn't be surprised."

Taylor wouldn't have been surprised, either. And she was happy for Doug, truly happy, but she wished Troy would call. She wanted to hear from him...unless they were finished and in that case, well, she'd want to know that, too.

Troy phoned right at the end of the Tuesday Night Book Group and it was the perfect excuse to step out of the room while Maureen and the others packed up their books and thermoses and pulled on their coats.

"Hey," she said, dropping her voice as she squeezed past the ladies to reach the door and step into the hall.

"Am I interrupting?"

"It's a good interruption. The Tuesday Night Book Group is just ending."

"I thought the meeting would be over by now."

"They talk *a lot*."

He laughed, a low husky sound that sent shivers of pleasure through her. "Haven't heard from you," he said. "Was getting worried. You okay?"

"Yes. Just busy. Tuesday is a long day." She hesitated, nervous, and then before she could stop herself, she blurted, "Are we okay?"

She could almost feel his smile.

"*We* are okay," he said cheerfully.

She flushed. "Why do you say it like that?"

"No reason."

"Hmph." She glanced behind her as the door to the meeting room opened and the ladies began to file out. She lifted a hand to acknowledge them but wasn't about to hang up on Troy, not after waiting days to talk to him. "I heard some good news today," she added.

"Oh, really?"

"I'm not supposed to know yet, but apparently Judge McCorkle is signing off on allowing Doug to live with me. He won't have to finish his probation at Hogue. That's wonderful, isn't it?"

"Yes, it is. That's fantastic news."

"It absolutely is. I need to go home and tell Doug. I haven't had a chance as I wanted to tell him in person."

"I'm sure he'll be relieved."

"He will be. So very much." She drew a breath. "Did you do this, Troy? Did you talk to the judge?"

"I didn't talk to McCorkle."

"Someone talked to him."

"I don't know."

"Troy."

"Sweetheart."

She giggled. "Did you really just call me sweetheart?"

"Yes, I did."

"That is so old fashioned."

"But you're a little bit old fashioned."

"Am I?"

"That's a compliment, Taylor."

"I don't know. Maybe we can find another one…something a little more modern. Like honey or baby."

"Or dude."

She burst out laughing. "That's awesome. Dude. Thank you."

"We'll work on endearments this weekend."

She said nothing, not sure what to say.

"Are you around this weekend?" he asked after a moment of awkward silence.

THE TYCOON'S KISS

"Yes," she said hesitantly. "Are you thinking of coming back this way already?"

"Dad's not well and I need to spend some time with him. Dillon needs his breaks, too. And then there is you. I'd very much like to see you, that is, if you want to see me—"

"Yes."

"You're sure, dude?"

She spluttered with laughter. "Yes, yes, yes. Come home this weekend. Please come see me."

"I've missed you, Taylor."

Her heart felt so full right then. It was a struggle to keep the emotion from spilling into her voice. "I've missed you, too."

"I have to warn you, I hate long distance. I have a rule about long distance."

"What's that?"

"Don't do it. But I guess rules are meant to be broken, because I want to see if we can make this work."

"Yeah?"

"Yeah. So I am making you a promise now, that I intend to come home every weekend—"

"That's a lot of flying."

"—as long as I can be there, I will be there. And I hope you know by now, that I don't make promises lightly. I don't make a promise that I don't intend to keep."

She didn't say anything for a moment, overwhelmed.

"But I don't want you to feel pressure," he added. "Dad

doesn't have much time left, and I need to spend time with him, so if at any point this isn't working for you—"

"Let's not go there yet," she breathed. "Let's just take it one weekend at a time. Right now, I'm just really looking forward to the next date. So Saturday?"

"You don't want to have dinner Friday?"

Taylor smiled slowly. "I'd love dinner Friday. Saturday, too, but I know you have other commitments and people you need to see in Marietta besides me."

"But there's no one I want to see more."

# Chapter Thirteen

JUST AS HE'D promised, Troy flew back from California to Montana every Friday from February to March. He was there in Marietta when his father died mid March, and he remained for a week after, helping Dillon with arrangements and then staying for the family only graveside services.

But after the service was over, Harley Sheenan, Brock's new wife had all the Sheenans to Copper Mountain Ranch for a big meal and Troy invited Taylor to join him, but she declined, thinking it wasn't the best time to meet everyone and she wasn't sure if she offended Troy or it was just the timing of everything, but when he returned to San Francisco the next day, he didn't come back to Marietta the following weekend, or the weekend after, and even though they talked on the phone daily, Taylor was uneasy.

She wanted to tell him she hadn't declined the invitation to hurt him, but to protect his family and respect their need to grieve without a stranger there.

Several times she opened her mouth, the words right

there on the tip of her tongue, but for some reason she couldn't bring it up.

But if he didn't come home this next weekend, she didn't know what to think.

For a month he'd been there every weekend, and she'd gotten used to seeing him every five days, and it had been so nice when he was in Crawford County the week following his dad's death because they'd seen each other every day.

It'd felt right to see him daily...lunches, dinners, and then the one night when Kara told her she'd keep an eye on Doug if Taylor wanted to stay overnight with Troy at the hotel.

Taylor did stay, and she and Troy had finally made love. They'd waited a month from the ball and she was glad they'd waited. It had been better than good. It had been amazing. Not just physically, but emotionally. If Taylor hadn't fallen in love with Troy before, making love cemented it. She was crazy about him. Head over heels. And yet now that she wanted him and needed him he was far away, staying away.

It was getting to her, too. Making her feel panicked and anxious and pessimistic...

Had he only wanted to sleep with her? Or had she been a disaster in bed? Was he disappointed?

He'd said she was wonderful and a good lover but he might have said that just to keep her from getting all emotional on him...

Maybe she needed to get a book on lovemaking tips.

THE TYCOON'S KISS

There were plenty out there. The library even had a few. There were old ones—Kama Sutra kind of things—but surely she could pick up a few pointers.

Taylor brought the Kama Sutra book home with her from work on Wednesday, intending to read it after dinner. But first, she needed to get dinner going.

She prepared the small roast and put it in the oven and then started some laundry and then returned to peel and chop potatoes and tear lettuce for a salad.

The potatoes were cooking nicely when Doug entered the kitchen. "Do you have a second?" he asked.

She'd just opened the oven door to check the roast. "Yes, of course."

She closed the oven and straightened. He looked wary which made her wary. "Everything okay?"

"Yes."

"What's up?"

"I have a job," he said gruffly.

Taylor pulled off the oven mitts. "What?"

"A job," he repeated, smiling crookedly.

"Doug, that's *good*." She hugged him. "That's great!"

"Tay, but wait. It means I wouldn't live here anymore—"

"No. Doug. *No*." She stepped back, squeezed his arms. "You can't move. You have to live with me. It's part of your probation. After the end of May you can do anything, but right now, no."

"Give me a chance to explain."

"There's nothing to explain." She stepped back and crossed her arms over her chest to hide that her hands were shaking. She was so upset. So upset. How could he not understand the seriousness of this? "You don't want to end back up at Hogue. You don't want to lose everything you've gained. So many people have gone out of their way to help you—"

"Troy, you mean," he interrupted.

"Yes, Troy!" Her voice broke. "And I'm not trying to rub your nose in it but—"

"Then don't, and there's no reason to be angry." He paced away from her, and then paced back, dragging his hand through his hair, rifling it. "If you'd just listen to me, Tay. Listen. Okay? You're getting all cray-cray."

"I just don't want you back where we were a few months ago."

"We won't be. I won't be." He drew a deep breath. "I'd still be in the area and it's okay. Judge McCorkle has said it's okay. He approves the job, and best of all, I'll be making some money. Not a lot, but enough to make it easier on you. You won't have to pay for everything from now on. I'll be able to take care of myself."

He was smiling at her, his expression earnest and hopeful and it made her feel so many different emotions. "What are you going to do?" she asked.

"I'm going to be working at the Copper Mountain Ranch. Working for Brock Sheenan. I'll live in the bunk-

THE TYCOON'S KISS

house and I'll get paid twice a month, just like he pays all his other hands. It's not much more than minimum wage but Brock said if I prove myself, then he can bump it up a bit."

He was talking quickly. He was happy, and proud and so very excited, which made her hopeful, and proud, too. "This is great news, Doug."

"I know. And I want you to know that I didn't ask Troy to get me a job, just to introduce me to a few people, if he didn't mind, and he didn't. He made some calls and told me to use him as a reference and then when no one had an immediate opening anywhere, he put me in touch with Brock. And now I have a job, and a place to live, and I'm not going to screw this up, I promise, Tay."

Taylor's heart thudded harder. She didn't quite know what to make of the mention of Troy, but she wasn't surprised. Troy had a way of working quietly behind the scenes, moving mountains, shifting paradigms…

"I know you'll do your best," she said huskily. "And that's all I've ever asked. Just do your best, and if you need help, let people know. Give people a chance to help you, when you need a hand, because you don't have to do it all on your own—"

"That's exactly what Troy said. About you." Doug grinned. "That you're pretty much perfect except for being stubborn and not good about asking for help. He said it's not a weakness to accept help now and then. If anything, it's a strength, to know your limitations." Doug made a face.

"Or something like that."

"How often do you talk to Troy?"

"We don't really talk. We just text."

"You do?"

He nodded. "A couple times each week, or whenever something comes up."

"I didn't know."

Doug hesitated, suddenly troubled. "You don't mind, do you?"

"No."

"He's really nice, Tay. And not condescending nice. Just…cool."

"That's good."

He nodded. "You can tell he has brothers. That's kind of how he treats me. Like a younger brother."

She went to the stove, turned down the heat beneath the boiling potatoes. "And you like that?" she asked, trying to hide the tears filling her eyes.

"Yeah. Sounds kind of corny but it makes me feel good, knowing he cares. Knowing I can ask him things, especially since I can't ask Dad and you're a woman. Not that it's bad to be a woman but you know…you're not a man."

She couldn't hold the tears back. They were falling, spilling onto the lid covering the potatoes, and then onto her hand. "No offense taken," she said, trying to stop the tears but it was a futile task.

Doug approached her, and patted her back awkwardly.

THE TYCOON'S KISS

"Tay, don't cry. Please, don't."

She just shook her head.

"But why are you crying?" he persisted. "What did I do? What did I say wrong?"

"Nothing."

"Then what's going on?"

She turned around and hugged him, hard. "I love you, Doug. And I'm happy you're happy."

"That's why you're crying?"

Taylor struggled to catch her breath. "Yes."

"You're sure?"

"Yes."

"Okay. Then maybe you might want to stop crying because it's kind of embarrassing, especially with Troy here. I don't know how he feels about tears but in general, guys find it a little weird."

Taylor jerked her head up and yes, there Troy was, standing in the kitchen door, his coat unbuttoned over a suit, a little bit of scruff on his handsome jaw.

She pulled back and scrubbed at her cheeks. "When did you arrive?"

"Just a second ago." Troy glanced from Taylor to Doug and back again. "Everything okay?"

"Yes." Taylor just stared at him, drinking him in. "Yes. If we're okay."

Doug ducked out of the kitchen, leaving them alone.

"Taylor, I love you. We better be okay."

217

SOME OF THE problems at work eased, and for the next month Troy was able to return to Marietta every weekend. It wasn't always easy for him to get away. Sometimes he spent the full day each weekend in Marietta tackling business headaches, but at least he was home for the weekend and he could take Taylor out to dinner, and back to the hotel.

He'd just arrived back in Montana late this afternoon and he and Taylor had picked up Doug from Copper Mountain Ranch and had taken him to dinner at a little barbecue place in Emigrant Gulch.

But it was close to ten now, and Doug was back at the bunkhouse and Troy and Taylor had arrived at the Graff. Troy handed the car and keys over to valet, and he and Taylor crossed the lobby, hand in hand.

"You're quiet," Taylor said, shooting him a swift glance. "Tired?"

"A little," he said, flashing her a smile. He was more than a little tired but he wasn't going to complain. He was a lucky man, and he knew it.

"Busy week?" she asked, wrapping her arms around him as they waited for the elevator.

"It was." He kissed her, and then again, suddenly hungry for her, and the quiet of his suite. Sometimes the only thing that got him through a grueling week where he was on and off planes, in and out of meetings, sleeping at a different hotel every night, was knowing that on Friday he'd be on a flight, heading east to see her.

As they walked down the hall to the suite, she gave his fingers a squeeze. "We don't have to go to the Spring Gala at Emerson's tomorrow night. We can just stay in, relax."

"You've been looking forward to the barn dance for weeks," he said, opening the door to his suite and turning on lights.

"There will be other dances."

"Not for the Great Wedding Giveaway." He tossed his outer coat onto the kitchen island and then drew off his blazer and unbuttoned the top three buttons on his shirt.

She went to him and helped him unbutton the rest of his shirt. "I'd rather be with you."

He smiled. "You will be with me. Dancing in a barn."

She laughed and he scooped her up into his arms and carried her into the bedroom. They kissed for what seemed like hours and then made love, a hot fierce coming together that left them sated and sleepy.

Taylor snuggled against Troy, so relaxed, perfectly content. "Amazing," she whispered.

He wrapped his arm around her, holding her to him. "Who would have ever thought that Marietta's new librarian was such a wild thing in bed?"

She gurgled a laugh. "I don't know how wild I am. You're the one with all the moves, and oh do you have some moves."

"I dig your body. But then, I'm pretty crazy about you."

And then they were kissing again, and loving again, because the weekends were always too short and Troy was always arriving just to say goodbye again.

It was early in the morning when Taylor opened her eyes. She felt deliciously warm, and loved. Cherished.

Troy was so good at making her feel secure, and safe.

He was so good at making sure she knew she mattered.

She looked up at him and discovered he was also awake and he was watching her. "Hey," she whispered.

"Hey, baby."

She stretched to press a kiss to his lips. "I love you."

She saw a flicker in his eyes and then his lips slowly curved. It was the first time she'd told him. She'd wanted to tell him. But it had never seemed right. It was right now. He should know. He ought to know. He'd changed her world, changed her.

"I just love you," she repeated. "That's all."

MUCH LATER THAT morning, after room service had delivered a delicious brunch with champagne right to their room, they ate their feast in bed and toasted the weekend—and each other—with the flutes of champagne.

"This is pretty decadent," Taylor said, grinning.

"In San Francisco everyone goes out on the weekend for brunch," he said. "I don't know if it's the weather, or just a West Coast thing, but brunch is big."

"I had no idea."

"I'd love for you to come to San Francisco for a week.

THE TYCOON'S KISS

It's a great city. We could drive to Napa or head down the coast to Monterey and Carmel."

"When?"

"Sunday night when I return. Come for the week. We can fly out together, spend the week in the Bay Area, and then have you back the following Sunday in time for work Monday."

"I wish I could."

"Why can't you?"

"Doug."

He leaned forward, kissed her. It was meant to be a quick reassuring kiss, but the moment her lips touched his, he just wanted more. That was the thing about her. It didn't matter how much he had of her, it was never enough.

When the kiss finally ended, he stroked her flushed cheek. "What about Doug?"

"I worry about him."

"I know you do, but Taylor, he's a young man—" Troy saw her lips part in protest and he added firmly, "—on his way to becoming a mature man and he can handle you being gone for a week. It's good for both of you to have some independence, and you can rest easy knowing he's at Brock's and nothing's going to happen to him there. Everybody in the bunkhouse will keep an eye out for him, and there's no one more maternal than Harley. She's one of five kids herself. She'll take good care of Doug. You know that."

"I do," she said in a small voice.

But she was still resistant. Still worried. "What else?" he asked.

"My job."

"Will be waiting. No one's going to fire you over taking a few days off, and good grief, wouldn't it be nice to miss one week of that horrible Tuesday Night Book Group?"

Taylor giggled and then her giggle turned to a heavy sigh. "But Maureen will talk. The *gossip*."

"And if it's not Maureen, then it will be Carol Bingley, who used to gossip about all us Sheenan boys. But what I've learned is that even if you don't go, or do anything bad, those same folks will talk anyway. It's not personal. It's just what they do."

She stifled another sigh. "True."

He smoothed her long dark hair back from her face, kissed her bare shoulder. He'd loved it when she'd giggled a moment ago. She sounded so young and carefree and it made his heart lift, happy. He'd never met anyone he'd wanted to make laugh the way he wanted to make Taylor laugh. He'd never met anyone he'd wanted to love the way he wanted to love her.

Taylor Harris deserved the sun and the moon.

And Troy Sheenan was damned determined to give her the sun and the moon and all the stars in the sky, too.

"I love you, Taylor." He kissed her again. "And if you're not ready to leave Marietta yet, that's okay. San Francisco will always be there. You come see my world there when

THE TYCOON'S KISS

you're ready."

She was silent a long moment. "Is that where you'd want to raise your kids… in the city?"

An interesting question, one he hadn't asked himself before but now that she'd put it to him… no.

He didn't want to raise his kids in a big city. He'd want to raise them here, in Marietta. "I think my kids would have to be raised in Montana. With you here, it once again feels like home."

She sat up, pulling the sheet with her. "You'd live on the Sheenan Ranch?"

"No. We'd find our own place." He saw her eyes widen at the use of *we*. "Preferably a big house on Bramble Lane," he added, tugging on a long strand of her dark silky hair. "That way during the summer our kids could walk to the library to see their mom."

Taylor blinked hard, her eyes turning liquid. "Are you saying what I think you're saying?"

"I want to marry you, Taylor." He hesitated a moment, and smiled crookedly. "I couldn't imagine any woman more perfect for me."

She knocked away the tears. "And you wouldn't mind if I wanted to work after we got married and had kids?"

"Of course not. You're my book girl. How could I take you away from what you love most?"

"But maybe I love you most," she said softly.

"That's a good answer." Smiling, he reached out to catch

the next tears before they could fall. "But there is no reason you can't have a family and do the work you love. I believe in you, Taylor. I believe you should be who you want to be. If you want to continue at the library, I'm one hundred percent behind you. If you want to work part-time, then that's what you should do. And if you want to stay home, I'm good with that, too. But I love you too much, and respect you too much, to make life decisions for you."

"You are one evolved man, Troy Sheenan," she whispered, leaning over to kiss him.

He pulled her down on top of him, kissing her back, tasting the salt of her tears. "My mother taught me well."

"I wish I could have met her, Troy."

"I wish you could have, too. She would have loved you. You would have been the daughter she never had."

"I hope we have a little girl. We could name her after your mom."

"I hope we have a little girl, and I hope she looks just like you."

"But without the big glasses."

"I'd love it if she wore big glasses. It'll help keep all the boys away."

Taylor punched him lightly in the shoulder. "I thought you said you loved me in glasses."

"I do. But as you know, I'm highly evolved."

Taylor didn't know whether she should laugh, cry or punch him again. "So most boys don't like girls who wear

THE TYCOON'S KISS

glasses."

"Well, we both know that most boys are fools. Let's just say *I* personally think book girls should rule the world."

She laughed and kissed him. "You are so good with words."

"I mean every word I say." He clasped her face in his hands, and kissed her slowly, thoroughly, completely. "I love you, Taylor, and I want to have a life with you, and read books with you—"

"Read books?"

"Sssh. I'm not finished. And take walks with you, and travel to interesting places with you, and make beautiful babies with you, and grow old with you. How does that sound?"

"Quite nice, actually," she said, smiling and snuggling closer. "I approve the plan. And I suggest we move forward. Immediately."

## THE END

From *New York Times* Bestselling author
Jane Porter comes…

## THE TAMING OF THE SHEENANS SERIES

If you enjoyed *The Tycoon's Kiss*, you will love the rest of the Sheenan brothers!

### Christmas At Copper Mountain

Book 1: Brock Sheenan's story

### The Tycoon's Kiss

Book 2: Troy Sheenan's story

### The Kidnapped Christmas Bride

Book 3: Trey Sheenan's story

### The Taming of the Bachelor

Book 4: Dillion Sheenan's story

### A Christmas Miracle for Daisy

Book 5: Cormac Sheenan's story

### The Lost Sheenan's Bride

Book 6: Shane Sheenan's story

*Available now at your favorite online retailer!*

# About the Author

New York Times and USA Today bestselling author of fifty romance and women's fiction titles, **Jane Porter** has been a finalist for the prestigious RITA award five times and won in 2014 for Best Novella with her story, *Take Me, Cowboy*, from Tule Publishing. Today, Jane has over 12 million copies in print, including her wildly successful, *Flirting With Forty*, picked by Redbook as its Red Hot Summer Read, and reprinted six times in seven weeks before being made into a Lifetime movie starring Heather Locklear. A mother of three sons, Jane holds an MA in Writing from the University of San Francisco and makes her home in sunny San Clemente, CA with her surfer husband, Ty Gurney, his vintage cars and trucks, and their two dogs.

Visit Jane at JanePorter.com.

Thank you for reading

## THE TYCOON'S KISS

If you enjoyed this book, you can find more from all our great authors at TulePublishing.com, or from your favorite online retailer.